THREAD TRAVELLER

ANNABEL YOUENS

PUBLISHED WORLDWIDE BY SALT LINE PRESS, 2025
COPYRIGHT © 2025 ANNABEL YOUENS

ALL RIGHTS RESERVED UNDER INTERNATIONAL AND PAN-AMERICAN COPYRIGHT CONVENTIONS. NO PART OF THIS BOOK MAY BE REPRODUCED IN ANY FORM OR BY ANY ELECTRONIC, ARTIFICIAL INTELLIGENCE OR MECHANICAL MEANS, INCLUDING INFORMATION STORAGE AND RETRIEVAL SYSTEMS, WITHOUT PERMISSION IN WRITING FROM THE PUBLISHER.

LIBRARY AND ARCHIVES CANADA CATALOGUING IN PUBLICATION
TITLE: THREAD TRAVELLER / ANNABEL YOUENS.
NAMES: YOUENS, ANNABEL, 1976-AUTHOR
DESCRIPTION: FIRST EDITION
IDENTIFIERS: CANADIANA | ISBN 978-1-0695122-1-5 (E-BOOK) | 978-1-0695122-0-8 (SOFT COVER) | 978-1-0695122-3-9 (HARDCOVER)

COVER DESIGN AND PAINTING: HANNAH SCHICKEDANZ
PRINTED IN CANADA, 1ST PRINTING

To my family—blood and found—for believing I could write this novel.

ONE
AUGUST

Exhausted and hungry, August sat on the floor of the Heathrow Airport by baggage carousel number thirty-four. *Do not think about the germs. Do not think about the germs... connect... just connect, damn it,* August mumbled as she tried to connect to the Heathrow WiFi.

August leant against a wall, with her legs outstretched and, her Apple laptop on her knees. The whole setup was precarious, with speeding feet and out-of-control luggage constantly hurtling past.

It's okay that 230,000 travellers visit Heathrow every day. You can have a shower when you get to your aunt's. That's probably five hours from now. Fuck.

August pulled hand sanitizer from the front pocket of her backpack and squeezed a huge glob onto her palm. She slathered it on her hands and wrists, inside her cardigan's cuffs. *Add to the list: Must order new refill of hand sanitizer from Nezza Naturals.*

"Mum, I really, really, really have to go to the bathroom," squealed her six-year-old daughter, bouncing by her feet. "I've gotta go *now*!"

August watched the WiFi connection "establish," willing it to finally connect. If she didn't see the contract changes by the end of the day, they'd have to pay their lawyers extra billable hours, more money they didn't have. All she needed was five minutes of internet!

With a sudden sharp pain in her shin, August looked up at her glaring daughter. "I HAVE TO GO RIGHT NOW," said Ripley.

August scanned the baggage area for her husband, huffing a deep breath. Of course, Andrew would disappear and leave her to handle everything. What else was new? She looked at her daughter. "Did you kick me?"

"Sorry, Mum. I wanted to get your attention."

She took another deep breath, "Okay."

She folded her laptop, standing on achy, long-haul legs. She scanned again, *Where the fuck is Andrew?* They couldn't leave their bags. August could see the scene unfold: British military police rushing, machine guns banging against their legs, their family hauled off for questioning and fines in British pounds, which would be a horrible exchange to their Canadian dollars.

"Get your backpack on," said August firmly.

"I don't want to."

"You have to. We can't leave our luggage unattended... Oh my God, just put it on."

Ripley pouted as she put on her backpack and grabbed the small wheelie bag.

Fuck, I'm never going to get this done. With one backpack over each shoulder and dragging the carry-on that *just fit* in the overhead bin, she quickly scurried to the washrooms with her daughter, circumventing piles of unclaimed luggage.

AT THE RENTAL CAR BOOTH, THINGS WERE NOT smooth. Immigration, baggage, and customs had taken almost an hour, and now the car rental teenager was on the phone with his supervisor, pushing his bright orange bangs out of his eyes. Someone else took her booked rental car. August watched the boy continuously sweep his fringe to the side, mumbling on the phone in a thick northern accent, "But I can't see that tab." *OMG, just cut your freaking bangs.*

Her phone dinged. She saw a message from her bestie, Tabatha, no doubt cosy on her sofa with her cat, Gizmo, sipping a cup of morning coffee.

> **TABATHA**
> Did you arrive safely?
>
> **AUGUST**
> Yep – we're here. It's a nightmare at Heathrow. I'm just trying to get the rental car. Text later.

"Mum, I'm hungry."

August looked at her six-year-old and considered giving up. Perhaps if she had a breakdown right now, they'd cart her off to a quiet room. *I'm sure they handle many mental health crises here, right? Add to the list: Book couples coun-*

selling session. Her daughter leant against her hip. "I need you to stop doing that, Ripley. I can't have anyone or anything else touch me right now."

Ripley pulled back, crossed her arms, and stared. "Andrew… " said August as she turned away from the ginger teen and Ripley. He stood across the hallway on his phone, as removed as a business traveller. *Fuck. Of course*, she thought.

"Andrew, I need you to handle this," she snapped, her voice barely audible over the rolling trolley wheels and other whining children.

Andrew looked up from his phone and grimaced. "I was *just* reading the lawyer's comments," he said. "There is no need to snap at me," he snapped back.

August rolled her eyes and considered taking her own life with her passport, by slicing herself in the neck. "Fine," said Andrew sharply. "Ripley, let's go."

Ripley smiled at her dad, glared at August, and walked across the hallway to take his hand. August and her baggage were alone. Tightness caught in her throat as a river of sweat trickled between her shoulder blades, settling into the band of her bra. The heat and weight of the day poured out of her body. *Fucking perimenopause.*

"Okay, we've got you sorted," said the teenager in a Budget blazer. With a final flick of his ginger bangs he said, "We've found you a nice minivan."

Great. A fucking minivan for the country roads of Kent. Jesus suffering fuck.

AUGUST

In the pouring rain of Budget lot twelve, August rooted around her suitcase, standing under the raised trunk of the minivan. The sweat on her body cooled, turning to chills. "Where the fuck is my rain jacket?" she said out loud.

She rifled more furiously through her vacation clothes. The trunk of the minivan mostly kept her dry, but wet dribbles hit the backs of her calves and rolled down into her New Balance runners. The heat and heaviness rose into her throat again. Her flustered fingers throbbed, and a headache was coming on. *Christ, I didn't drink enough water on the plane. Add to the list: Order a new straw for Ripley's water bottle.*

"Hey, did you send through my comment about the security review in section five point two?" asked Andrew in an annoyed tone from the front passenger seat.

"Mum, where is my plug for my iPad?" asked Ripley as she stared out the window into the parking lot, glassy eyes of a child who had slept very little on the flight from Vancouver.

August picked up her suitcase and flipped it over, dumping all her clothes, shoes, toiletries, underwear, and socks in the trunk. Her legs vibrated. "Where the fuck is my rain jacket?"

"What about the comment?" asked Andrew louder, swivelling around to look at August through the length of the van.

"Muuuuuuuummmmmm" Ripley whined, her chin on the back of the seat, staring with exasperated eyes.

"NO! I don't know where your iPad charger is and, YES, Andrew! While I was taking our daughter to the bathroom, dragging all our luggage around, and getting a fucking minivan, I did somehow find the time to send through your comments to the lawyer. I did all that, plus packed everyone for this trip and somehow forgot my OWN FUCKING RAIN JACKET!"

August slammed the minivan trunk down with an unsatisfying click, looking up at the rain clouds. The drops fell on her fiery face. "ARGGHHHH," she screamed.

Standing by her Citroën SpaceTourer minivan, August felt her female ancestors yell in solidarity. *I wish Tabatha was here.* August imagined Tabatha finding the iPad charger, getting Ripley settled with a snack, and making her laugh. Women helping women with no need to be asked.

As the shaking stopped, she looked into the minivan's rear window. Ripley's eyes welled with tears. Andrew simmered with contempt. *What a great start to our fucking holiday. This is going to be a wonderful family trip to see my aunt.*

TWO
AUGUST

August lay on the bed in her aunt's guest room when her phone buzzed with a message.

TABATHA

I'm so sorry it's been a rough start. Go clean up and you'll feel better.

AUGUST

You're right. I need to get out of these gross plane clothes.

TABATHA

Plane clothes. Ew.

AUGUST

Okay, I should stop hiding in the bedroom, Andrew's being an ass about the contract and of course the deal is still not done.

TABATHA

Yikes, that sounds nasty. I hope you can both get the sale closed.

AUGUST

> Me too! I'm so fucking over this. Talk later. xo

It had taken over three hours to get to her aunt's house in Kent. The roads hadn't been too busy, and she'd driven all of the roundabouts in the right direction. *I'll take that win.*

Her mouth was dry, her jaw like concrete, eyes heavy and hot. She took a deep breath. She could hear Andrew and Ripley chatting with her aunt in the kitchen. *Likely talking about what a bitch I've been*, she sighed.

August stripped off her long-sleeve shirt and shrugged down her sweatpants. She tore off her socks, noticing the horizontal bands where the sock elastic pressed against her shins. She rubbed the indents softly, quickly standing as Andrew flung open the door and strode into the bedroom. "Did you update that final paragraph?"

"Yes." *Breathe, August, just stare out the bedroom window and breathe.*

"Did you put the disclosure clause in there?"

"Yes." *Breathe again.*

"Did you find out what the outstanding share meant?"

"I have an email in to the lawyer," said August. *Breathe even more...*

"And did the – "

"Oh my God, did you even *read* my email!" August yelled, looking down at her feet, the peeling blue polish on her toes. *Add to the list: Book a pedicure so my feet don't look so gross.*

She didn't need to look up to recognise Andrew was

tense, the two of them falling into a hardened and familiar pattern. "I just wanted to confirm this, August. You know this is important, right?" asked Andrew with a sneer.

The sarcasm crept up her throat. She couldn't stop it. "No. I have no idea how important it is. I'm completely oblivious to the fact we need to sell our company so we don't lose our house."

"Jesus, August. This is why you're so hard to talk to," muttered Andrew, striding out of the room. He slammed the door with more style than sound, a houseguest door slam.

August threw herself on the bed, rolling into her pillow, and screamed, "MOTHERFUCKER!"

AUGUST SAT ON THE BED, HER SKIN WET AFTER A tepid British bath, when Andrew came back into the guest room. During her soak, August had gathered herself up. *You need to apologize and try to calm things down. This is going to be an awful holiday if you don't rein this in.*

Andrew sat on the edge of the bed and faced the window of the Kentish countryside. Fog hung across the garden, a sign it was hopping season, time to harvest the acres of beer hops that decorated this region. With a calm voice, to the foggy world outside, Andrew said, "You know, we only have six months left of funds. If we can't close this deal, we won't be able to pay our staff or our mortgage and we'll likely lose the house."

August gritted her teeth, "I know," she said as softly as she could.

"So if you know that, why can't you answer me civilly? We have to get our comments back to the lawyer. This is *it*. We can save ourselves if we get this purchase done."

"I know," August repeated.

It was quiet for a bit. They both stared at the fogged woods and watched the orange sunset slowly change to pink. Selling the tech company they'd cofounded twelve years ago was exactly how their family was going to survive. That's why she couldn't stand it; the pressure made her bones ache. She relaxed her jaw, a hollow opened in her throat. "We're on holiday and I want us to have a good time, but there's always work getting in the fucking way."

Andrew stood up, turned to look at her, and rubbed his hand across the top of his tightly shaven head. "Oh, Christ, August. I wanted to cancel the trip but you said it would be fine. We could 'do the holiday and get the deal done'. You always make everything out to be so easy, but it's not!"

They were silent for a while, Andrew's back outlined against the fig tree training up the garden trellis. "Are you ready to have an actual conversation without getting snippy?" said Andrew.

Breathe and unclench your jaw. Be the model of diplomacy. "Look, let's go help Bonnie get dinner ready, have a proper meal that isn't salted peanuts and a ginger ale, then we can sit down to review the contract and email together. Sound good?"

She waited for Andrew's reply. *He must finish his current thought before he can answer my question.* It was a test of her willpower to remain quiet.

"Fine," he said flatly.

August understood "fine" meant "fine," but right now "fine" was a bomb. *Just be cool, August. Just stay cool. You got this.* She rolled her eyes and left before things got worse. *Okay, it's time to put on my "I'm having the best time ever on my family holiday although everything is going to total shit" face,* she told herself as she padded down the hallway to help her aunt make the dinner salad.

After dinner, followed by two strong gin and tonics, Ripley asked for a dance party. August's seventy-two-year-old aunt, in her black Chelsea boots, black skinny jeans, and loose black sweater, mimicked six-year-old Ripley's dance moves around the living room. The immense black-framed windows mirrored the dizzy couple twirling in the late evening light.

Andrew leant against the wall, managing the playlist, tapping his foot. The two generations enjoying "Let's Dance," channelling powerful Bowie energy. Andrew's phone dinged, and a warmth rose in August's throat. Andrew looked sternly at his phone, then the three channels on his forehead deepened as he looked up at August with the all too familiar "grimace."

August expected the "grimace" from the family in her life. Before the trip, August visited her mum for a cup of tea, a digestive biscuit, and a catch-up. Her mum sat in her gardening clothes, an old blue hiking top and pants that were slightly baggy where the elastic was stretched out.

The "grimace" arrived as her mum picked up her mug and said, "This hasn't worked out to be the best-timed trip, has it?"

Every muscle in August's body tingled, her nervous system ramping up to deflect and defend. "No," she sighed. "Everything is up in the air with the deal, but we booked this trip months ago on sale, so there's no turning back," she replied.

"You and Andrew have so much on your shoulders. You've both worked so hard for so long."

"I honestly don't know what it would be like to live without stress," August said with a slight chuckle.

"I just worry about you, that's all."

"Yes, Mum. But we're fine. We're really hoping the deal closes soon, ideally before we board the plane."

"I hope so too, sweetheart, because there have been other deals and they haven't worked..."

August cut her off and said, "Mum. I know that."

After a slight pause, her mum said, "Okay, I just want you to be looked after."

"Mum, I can look after myself. I don't need Andrew or anyone else to do that. Okay?" August said, ramping up her volume.

"All right, I'm sorry I said anything," retorted her mother, in her strong British accent. She continued, "You've always been so independent, even as a child. After the adoption was finalized, you resisted calling us Mum and Dad for years."

There was silence while August roared with anger. *Jesus, she's always got to bring up the adoption.* A hummingbird flitted at the window, sipping from the feeder. *Maybe that's the secret, liquid sugar for never-ending energy. Add to the list: Put more simple syrup in the feeder, so the hummingbirds don't die while we're on holiday.*

"Well, I'd better get going," said August, lightening the mood. "I've got the last couple things to pack for tomorrow. Plus, I've got a load of laundry to get on."

"You've still got laundry to do?" said her mother, looking slightly shocked. "I would've been packed last week."

"Yep, I know you would," sighed August as she stood up and rallied herself for the never-ending list of things to do she carried with her.

"I love you, sweetheart. You're my daughter and I just want you to be happy," said her mum as she hugged August, smelling of earth.

August relaxed into the hug for a moment. "I love you too."

On the drive home August thought about all the things she was failing at, starting with an empty childhood when her birth parents abandoned her. She wondered if Andrew's nightmare would come true, the deal wouldn't close, they'd miss several mortgage payments, live in their Kia Soul with their six-year-old daughter and their two cats.

"August," said Andrew firmly.

"Oh, what, sorry," said August, mentally coming back to her aunt's living room.

"I said they want to change the period of my retention again. I thought we'd agreed on this!"

As Andrew stormed off to find his laptop, August realized something definitely had to change.

THREE
AUGUST

August sat on the edge of Ripley's twin bed. "Are you comfy in here, sweetheart?"

The room was normally Bonnie's study, but a soft twin mattress lay against one of the bookshelf walls. Her aunt's vast collection surrounded them, a biography of Georgia O'Keeffe, a collection of historical wallpaper from the V&A Museum, assorted novels.

August ran her hand over Ripley's forehead, pushing the blonde bangs out of her face. Ripley was adamant her hair had to be long. This meant teary afternoons watching *Bluey* while August wrestled with the knots and muttered under her breath about giving Ripley too many choices. *Add to the list: Order more detangler.* "I'm good in here, Mum. This bed is cozy."

"It is, isn't it? Auntie Bonnie did a lovely job making you a comfy space to sleep. And your dad and I are right next door if you need anything."

"Yep, I know."

"Want me to put your rain sounds on?"

"Yes, please."

August fiddled with the ancient iPhone that was Ripley's "rain machine" and audiobook phone.

"What rain do you want tonight, sweetheart?"

"I think 'Gentle River.'"

August selected "Gentle River" and set the timer for thirty minutes.

"Will you rub me?"

"Of course."

Ripley rolled onto her left side, facing the bookshelf, pulling up the right side of her unicorn pyjama top. August rubbed up and down Ripley's shoulder blades, and back around to her side in an oval. She gently dragged her nails over her daughter's soft skin. *How could any mother give their child up?* August couldn't handle that right now; the desperate compulsion to sell the company overwhelmed her brain. *But what if we actually sold the company?* For a second, she caught a glimmer of relief. A sale would mean security. It would mean happiness. It would mean not crossing your fingers at the grocery checkout when they run your card. It would mean more slices of joy in the house, and less arguments over the dinner table. It would mean happiness in the mornings, rather than fighting depression that demands you stay in bed. It would mean having friends over for dinner and not being a phoney when you say, "Everything is fine." It would mean feeling secure in your own house. It would mean not hiding your shame in a team meeting because you're worried about the next pay run. It would mean not waking up at 4:23 in the morning fretting your mortgage payment has bounced because it's the same day you get paid. It would mean eating less Subway and less vegetables rotting in the crisper drawer. It would mean not checking your emails first thing in the morning. It would mean not being woken up by midnight server alerts and watching your panicked husband freak out. It would mean cherishing your life, instead of loathing it. It would mean no more angry words last thing at night to her husband. It would mean being more patient when Ripley came home with an uneaten lunch bag. It would mean loving herself enough to look after herself, and not just everyone else. It would mean being whole. It would mean *everything*.

"Mum, what's wrong?"

August saw her daughter looking at her. "You stopped rubbing my back. What are you thinking about?"

"Oh, sorry, sweetheart. I just got wrapped up in my thoughts."

"Mum?"

"Yes."

"Are you happy? You seem sad, even though we're on holiday."

"Well, honestly your dad and I are a little distracted with work. But once that's done we'll feel so much better and more happy."

"Mum?"

"Yes."

"There's so much to be happy for. Every day there are the best surprises. And right now we're on holiday! We get to have ice cream *every day* when we're on holiday!"

August's stomach thawed a little, a small glow spread

from her chest. "You're right, sweetheart. Ice cream every day makes me happy."

August gave Ripley her final goodnight kiss and wished desperately that ice cream could *actually* melt her to-do lists away.

FOUR
AUGUST

"Do you think we can try to have a *tiny* bit of fun today?" August asked as she backed the minivan out of her aunt's ivy covered driveway. *Oh God why did I start the conversation like that? I didn't mean it to be quite so poisonous.*

"Seriously, that's how you're going to start our day out?" said Andrew, pulling out his phone.

August finished reversing the minivan down the long driveway, put it in park, and said, "Okay, I know. Fuck. I'm sorry."

She put the van in gear and entered the small country lane towards town. The skin on her left arm burst into annoying itches. She tried to scratch it into submission as the van veered into the high hedge, thrusting the side mirror into the scrappy branches. *Oh, Christ, I hope we get our deposit back. Add to the list: Double-check what's covered by our travel insurance.* August grimaced, waiting for Andrew to make a comment about her driving. Nothing.

The ancient church spire rose above a thicket of oak

trees. August pushed the button to open her window - a rush of air on her face, the scent of hopping season, warm sunshine, and earth. *Ah,* Canterbury Tales *land*. Without even looking over, she sensed Andrew was on his phone.

This landscape felt so familiar. Growing up August's British parents took her on several vacations to visit relations and friends in the UK. Sting's "Fields of Gold" played in her brain, the soundtrack for family road trips through Kent and Dorset.

These days, August still took to the road with her bestie, Tabatha. Although now it was cups of McDonald's coffee, if they were watching their budget, and a flat white if they could splurge. They puffed their weed vapes, while music blared from the RAV4. It was the only time she felt freedom, true freedom. She was just August; not a mum, or a wife, or a daughter... just herself. Just her and Tabatha with the salty sea air as they wound their way alongside the Pacific Ocean.

August drove the minivan past the front gates of the brewery. After a couple of difficult turns, and grunting from Andrew, August found a large spot to park the van. Grabbing her Bikini Kill tote bag, she checked her phone. Bonnie had offered to look after Ripley for the afternoon, so she and Andrew could have a date. *I wouldn't exactly call this a date. Is it a date when you want to...* She hopped out of the van ignoring her thoughts.

"So, we're just waiting on the final version from the New York lawyers, right?" Andrew finally spoke as he shut the van door.

"Yep. We should get the final copy tonight before we go to bed."

"And then it's done, I guess, but I won't count on it until everyone signs the paperwork."

August's stomach churned. *Can this really be happening? Will we be okay?* Andrew opened the wide wooden doors to the entrance of the Shepherd Neame brewery, hand-carved hops framed the entrance. *I wonder how this talk is going to go? Courage, mon ami!*

The pub filled August's nose with the scent of beer and they joined a group of six other couples at the bar, where the tour of Britain's Oldest Brewery was to begin. The tour guide arrived, with a small badge that said "Edward." In his early sixties, he had a bright smile and a short shock of white hair that almost stood upright. "Today I'm going to take you back in time to experience the rich history of this here brewery, the oldest brewery in Britain. We'll stroll through the gallery, watch a video from relatives of the founding family, and then I'll take you in to where the sausage (aka the beer) gets made. And finally, the best part of the entire tour, a sampling of our favourite ales. Alright, friends, this way."

The small group followed Edward towards a set of swinging doors around the corner from the pub area. The sign said, "Employees Only." As August stepped through the doors, she detected a slight tingle in her toes. *Probably fucking perimenopause... but I didn't know foot tingling was a symptom...*

Waiting like polite Canadians for their samples of beer, August and Andrew stood towards the end of the bar. Their tour group turned out to be a mix of mostly Brits, two Americans, and the two Canadians. August ran her hand along the bar, surprised it wasn't sticky. The whole pub was more like a home where friends met to connect. The scent of hops and malt took her right back to her bathtub brewing days at university.

August once lived in a giant character farmhouse with friends where they'd brewed their own beer in the fourth bathroom. They'd put a cardboard sign on the door that said "Get Pissed Brewery" in scruffy handwriting. Beneath that, underlined multiple times for impact: "Don't Mess with the Thermostat."

She'd spent more time washing beer bottles than actually brewing beer, but it had been great fun and, much to their surprise, their efforts were rewarded with drinkable, cheap beer. Andrew checked his email on his phone. "The document?" August asked.

"Nothing yet." Andrew sighed.

"And here you go, you lovely Canadians," said Edward from behind the bar and put down two platters with four generous tasters on each. "So working left to right we have the beer that made us famous, the Spitfire, which is a red ale, followed by a lager called the Misstate, a pale ale called Water's Edge, and one of the original recipes we've modernized slightly: it's a take on a pale ale sweetened with honey, called Five Bees. Enjoy, my friends."

August and Andrew both picked up their flights and moved to a small wooden table and chairs. They sat across from each other. "Oh man, do I need this," said August.

"You're not fucking joking," said Andrew.

August looked at Andrew, his eyes wide and sad. They clinked glasses and August waited for Andrew to make eye contact. August loved cheersing. It was a sign of respect, a brief moment you could say, "I see you and I appreciate you." Andrew always made cheeky, bulging eye contact because he knew how important a good cheers was to August. He bulged his eyes at her, she smiled, and they both said, "Cheers."

"Oh, that's delicious," said August.

Andrew murmured.

They both sat for a few moments, sipping their beer. August, as usual, scanned the room, watching the other couples, imagining their stories. Andrew had one hand on his brow, massaging the creases that took up residence.

"Do you think we're actually going to sell our company?" August asked, tentatively, like she was going to jinx the shutout.

After a careful pause, Andrew said, "I'd say it's about eighty percent done."

"I can't even really believe this," said August, biting her lip. "If we do sell, we won't end up living with my mum."

"Or living in the Kia," said Andrew, deadpan.

They both sighed. August took a deep, brave breath and said, "Or maybe we're not going to live together anymore," trying to make the idea of separation sound incredibly casual.

Andrew didn't look up at her, just kept sipping his lager and swiping at his phone. *Did he even hear me? Do I want to spend the rest of my life staring at the top of his head and his twitching fingers?*

August finished her red ale. *Let's switch gears*, she thought and said, "Now, which one next? Ah, pale ale, your time is up," she said, picking up the pale pint, and taking a sip. "Pretty nice, but I think I prefer the red."

Andrew looked at the bar, scanning the tap handles with a strained look on his face. *Okay, I don't enjoy this feeling. I know he's processing, but this idea of separation can't be a surprise. Okay, just change the subject. He needs more time.* "What was your favourite part of the tour?" August asked, like she hadn't just casually mentioned the end of their marriage.

Andrew didn't look up from his phone as he said, "I enjoyed seeing the brewing vats, how they use modern tech and traditional methods."

"Yeah, that was cool," said August, taking another sip of the Water's Edge. And since it didn't seem like Andrew was going to ask her what she'd enjoyed, she continued, "I didn't know that ale wives were the original brewers. Brewing is always framed as such a male profession." *Fucking patriarchy.*

August took a last sip of her pale ale and pulled her phone out. She thumbed it open. No messages from Bonnie or Tabatha. *I guess I'm not talking to anyone, anywhere, right now.* August looked at the other two beers and picked up the historical beer, Five Bees. The little card alongside read, "These hops come from the original field used to create this beer in 1438. Declared an area of historical significance by the Kentish Brewery Society, the name is said to come from five local women who raised hives in the county." August put the taster to her lips, touched the cool condensation on the glass, and took a large sip. "Oh man, that's delicious." The anxiety in her mind, a future divorce surged through August's body. *OH MY GOD, will he ever respond to me!*

She perceived a warming in her toes, like walking on a heated floor, comforting and safe. Then a huge flash of adrenaline shot through her body. Nausea rose from her stomach as her eyesight blurred. *Oh fuck. I'm having a heart attack. Add to the list: Make doctor's appointment and get a full physical.*

All she felt was a warm softness around her body and a deep connection to something – *Are you there god? It's me, August. Do you make jokes when you're dying? Is this another fucking perimenopause symptom, because if so, NO ONE told me about this.*

It was like swimming in a warm lake. She wasn't scared, or anxious, or even lonely. There was a deep-rooted calmness to her consciousness. *God, if only I could tap into this on a daily basis.*

August sensed nothing but a soft rushing sound in her ears that made her close her eyes. She breathed out and smiled at the white nothingness. *Well, if this is death, this is the loveliest, softest, and happiest way to die.*

FIVE
AUGUST

August opened her eyes. Her body ached like an extra who'd tumbled down the Sacré-Cœur steps in *John Wick 2*. *"Fuck,"* she said out loud as she moved her head. A sizzle of pain ran from her palms to her neck.

She stretched her jaw and smelt rich mushroom soup. Her tongue discovered rough patches inside her mouth. *Weird.*

August lay on her side and gradually pushed herself up, tilting her neck back and forth, the sizzles of tightness softening. *Fuck, I feel awful.*

Finally, taking in her view, August saw wooden logs arranged like mini mazes of timber. Something organic grew on various piles. *Where's the pub? Where's Andrew? Where am I?* August struggled to stand up, every joint aching. She squinted against the cold sun. An enormous field stretched out, hundreds of piled oak logs. *They're like tiny, very airy wood cabins. Where is this?* Grouped in piles, the logs crisscrossed, creating towers that reached to shoulder height. August touched the pile next to her, roughened bark with small holes drilled in regular lengths along each log.

As a gust of wind bit her back, she realized she was freezing. She looked down at her body. "What the hell is going on?" She wasn't wearing any clothes. *Oh shit, was I raped?* August recalled every British police procedural she'd seen showing women raped and left in fields to die. She hugged her arms around her body. Small pieces of red fungus clung to her arms. She brushed the scraps off, fear rising in her throat. *Whoa, let's not panic just yet.* August took a couple of deep breaths, pressing her hands to her groin. *No bruising or hotness; I'm okay.*

A flood of embarrassment swallowed her fear, reddening her cheeks. *Did I get super drunk and do something inappropriate?* She took a step and stumbled, her feet numb. Clenching her breasts with her arms, August imagined herself in the Pacific Ocean, cold-water dipping with Tabatha, their weekend ritual. "You're good at cold. You know it's only temporary. You can do this," she whispered to herself, scanning beyond the field of logs; a layer of mist evaporated as the sun peered through.

August leant against the tower of logs; the sun slowly warmed her. She closed her eyes. *Okay, when you open your eyes, you're going to be back at the pub. Three, two, one, open.*

The vast field of logs greeted her eyes, and so did a bumblebee the size of a squash ball. August stepped away from the enormous buzzing insect as it landed on a nearby log. With no interest in August, the bee picked at what looked like a deep red mushroom fruiting from one of the drilled holes. "Huh," said August and leant closer, the large patterned wings like rippled tissue paper.

August sighed, dropping the tension from her shoulders. *So, I don't think I'm dreaming... because when you dream, you don't actually know you're dreaming... so I'm hallucinating?* The fluffy bee lifted from the mushroom and flew off down the field. A welcome warmth fell on her body as the last of the morning fog vanished.

August, grateful for the heat, bathed in the sunshine, as a grasshopper the size of a stapler hung on to a clump of grasses. "Huh," said August again and moved to the insect, studying the massive leg hairs. She stumbled as the grasshopper jumped from the grasses and disappeared into a log stack. *Massive insects, piles of mushroom logs and I'm naked. Can I hallucinate myself naked?*

August took a few tentative steps between the rows of logs. She could finally feel the ground, warm under her feet, and a growing stability in her legs. With ginger steps, she continued down the sloped field, the pungent mushroom smell deepening as she travelled.

Eventually August reached the end of the logs, where the brush of a forest began. Here, a small path invited her to step into the tangled woods. *I hope I'm not hallucinating my death march, straight to the wicked witch's cottage.* August tried to laugh, but it came out as a nervous hiss. She shook her head and, with curiosity outweighing her fear, she stepped into the eerie forest.

THE CEDAR AND OAK FOREST THICKENED, GIVING off a warming damp-wood scent. She ducked under moss-covered branches and, at one point, slid over a giant root across the trail, a smooth track on the surface where others had slithered over the reaching limb. With her hand on the root, August followed its long tentacle back into the brush until she lost sight. Raising her head in its direction, she cried out loud, "Oh my God!" A massive oak tree the height of the Eiffel tower rose above the forest ceiling. *Add to the list: Book the arborist to assess the sickly cedar.* August stopped. *Why would I hallucinate massive insects and trees and also hallucinate items on my to-do list? What the actual fuck...*

She shoved her never-ending to-do list from her mind as a fly the size of a hummingbird raced past her ear. *Okay, now big flies, that tracks.* The path descended towards a stream and split in two separate ways. At the edge of the flow, as if it had waited, sat a muscular black cat with purple eyes, lavender wells with bright black pupils. "Well, aren't those the most beautiful cat eyes I've ever seen?" said August.

The cat twitched its ears, tilted its head, and then bent down to nuzzle an itchy spot on its paw, gripping a tuft of black fur with its jaw. The stream gurgled over the rocks, a coolness lifting from the water to August's body. August looked down at her wobbly thighs and remembered she was naked. Another large bee settled on a purple foxglove beside the stream. August wiggled her jaw, loosening her tight and anxious grip. The cat finished nuzzling, stood up, and sauntered down the path to the right. Unsure what to do, August called out, "I'm coming with you, cat."

AUGUST

The cat continued, tail held in the air as it effortlessly weaved along the sandy track beside the stream. *Well, if I hallucinated this cat, I guess I should follow it.*

August relaxed as she walked. Moving her body cleared her brain. Another squash ball bee dipped into an orange poppy at the foot of an oak tree. It bobbed and landed on the bushy black centre; it waded through the pollen, then lifted off like an overloaded craft. August smiled at the ambling bee and wondered if hallucinations were always so consistent.

The path opened into a small clearing with a cottage nestled up against the forest on the left; the dwelling appeared to be made of a spongy red brick.

August followed the cat through the field. She slowly made out a woman, *maybe late sixties*, sitting on a three-legged stool underneath a large oak. The woman, with great care, picked a small object from a wicker basket, plucked something tiny from its cup shape and placed the treasure in her green apron. The woman's bright grey hair rolled down her back and billowed over her shoulders like a silver cape. Soft wrinkles on her brow and grooves along her cheeks highlighted supple, glowing skin. *Wow, she's stunning.* A soft hum came from the woman's thin lips, a tune August didn't recognize.

Sunlight glinted off the woman's hair as she looked up from her work, a quizzical expression on her face. "Well, now, who've ya found, Hazel?" she asked the black cat as it rubbed against her skirt. "I've seen many a pilgrim, but never a naked one before. Have ya been bathing in fungi?" she asked, gesturing to August's body.

August looked down. "Ah, right? I'm naked. I promise I'm not dangerous." She paused a moment. "Honestly, I'm lost and hallucinating."

With a warm smile, the woman placed the small collection from her apron in the basket, and stood up, the green apron tickling her ankles. Her bare feet were solid, almost fused with the earth. "Ya're right there. Some days of this life do feel hazy. I heard through the Mother of a visitor, although this message was different... anyways, we should get ya some clothes." She put her hands on her hips, one hand resting on a small knife in a sheath on her belt, then looked August up and down again with soft eyes. "We can't have ya roaming around in ya birthing suit," the woman said, smiling, her lightly tanned skin stretching with her lips.

The woman walked with a limp on the right and opened the door to the cottage. August was grateful she hadn't hallucinated a band of blood-thirsty murderers and looked around the field. A small herbal garden with a woven fence protected the seedlings from hungry animals. "I don't have any underthings for ya, but at least we can cover ya top and bottom," said the woman, returning with a light green pile of cloth in her arms. "Put these on, lass," she said as she handed August a tunic top and what looked like a skirt with various ties.

August put the skirt on the ground while she slipped the tunic over her head; the light fabric smelt musky, of the earth. She picked up the skirt and studied the many fabric ties, confusing her fingers and brain. *Maybe I tie it from the front?* She fussed with the skirt, twisting the fabric, attempting some modesty. The ties slipped through her fingers and the skirt fell to the ground. She grit her teeth, her impatience rising, her confusion tiring. *Oh my God, this is not mission control, why is this skirt so complicated?* August looked up; the woman watched her curiously and said with a smile in her voice, "Ya having trouble there?"

"Yep, I have no idea what I'm doing," said August, a knot rising in her throat. "It all feels a bit much."

With purposeful steps, the woman strode over and gently spun the skirt and its ties to the back. Soft tugs and gentle hands tightened the skirt around August's waist. "My name's Margaret," said the woman behind her.

"My name's August."

"Ah, that's a fine name for ya and ya grand height," said Margaret. "Would ya like to rest a bit with me?" she asked as she pulled another stool over to her basket. "Care to help me remove the tiny bulbs from these butter nests? And perhaps ya can tell me how ya come to be covered in cosmos," she said, pointing to the red fungi clinging to August's arms and woven through her unravelling bun.

August put more bread in her mouth, as she realized just how hungry she was. *I'm surprised I didn't hallucinate chocolate, but Jesus, this bread is delicious. Add to the list: Listen to* The Body Is Not an Apology *on Audible... Oh August, just stop with the fucking list!* "Ya all right, August?" asked Margaret as she handed August another mug of ale.

"Yeah, I mean, No... but the food and drink are helping. Thank you, Margaret."

"Ya're most welcome, dear," said Margaret as she took a bite of bread.

The sun was high in the sky. "Is it midday?" asked August, shading her eyes with her hand.

"It is." And then she added, "Did ya happen to eat some fungi with deep purple rings?"

August thought for a moment. "No. This is the first thing I've eaten since I showed up."

"And ya don't remember arriving?"

"That's right. I was with my husband drinking beer in Faversham and suddenly I was here. Wherever here is."

"Well, ya're still near Faversham."

"What, I am?" August stood up excitedly. "Oh, I'm so glad! I can get back! I'm sure Andrew is worried sick, and Ripley, and my aunt. I've got to go!" August set her mug down on the stool, turned to the forest, then stopped. "Um... how do I get to Faversham?" asked August, looking back at Margaret.

Margaret laughed and said, "Ya head back along the way Hazel brought ya, then carry on down the stream. It'll lead ya to the town."

"Thanks," said August. "Of course I'll get these back to you," she said, patting down her clothes. "I'm sure you need them."

"Oh, lass. Ya need them more. We know ya'll carry on the kindness and should ya need us, we're here."

"Thanks again, Margaret," August said, waving, and headed for the path. The black cat slowly appeared in the shadow at the edge of the forest. "Thanks to you too, Hazel!" August said happily. The cat watched a few of her footsteps, then sprinted into the forest.

Now clothed, fed, and slightly buzzed from the ale, August lengthened her steps. Her eagerness to see Ripley rose with each footfall. Without noticing, August hummed the *Star Trek: Next Generation* theme as she headed back to her family, excited to share her curious adventure.

August arrived at the edge of the town, her big toe bleeding after she'd stubbed it on a tree root. Distracted from her injury, August stared at an immense tower looming over the village. *I don't remember seeing that in Faversham.*

Red dust from the woods covered her feet and ankles as she strolled into the town's core. All the dwellings had the same brick-like blocks of Margaret's cottage. August scanned the buildings for the Shepherd Neame brewery, those wide wooden doors with the carved hops announcing the entrance. A woman or, really, a girl, pushed young twin boys along the road with one hand and held a heavy cloth shopping bag in the other. "Excuse me," said August, "do you know where the Shepherd Neame brewery is?"

The woman barely glanced at August, "Sorry, luv, never

heard of it," and continued cajoling the boys, who kept stopping to throw rocks at each other, up the street.

August's toe ached, the pain deepening with every step. *Fuck, that hurts. Do I have something in it?* The pain pulsed up the right side of her leg. A wooden sign hung over a door: a red mushroom surrounded by overlapping silver circles. Relief flooded August as she sat down on a pile of bricks stacked up beside the doorway. She picked up her foot and placed it over her knee to inspect her toe. *Add to the list: Must do more pigeon pose; these hips are tight!*

A tall man rushed out of the building and stomped towards her yelling, "What the hell do ya think ya're doing?" He raised his hands and powerfully pushed August.

August tumbled from the bricks, her butt smacked by the hard ground. Eyes wide, she stared at the man as he continued yelling, "These cosmos bricks haven't cured, ya stupid woman! Ya'll distort them and I'll lose an entire week's work! I'm already behind to the guild!" With his last point made, he gurgled and spit in her face.

"What are you doing?" August exclaimed from the ground as she wiped the spit off her cheek, "I was just trying to check my bleeding toe!"

The man screwed up his mouth, "I don't care about ya stupid foot," then added, "Purification is the way of the Divine Sphere," then spun around, his leather apron flapping against his legs as he strode back into the building.

"Jesus," muttered August. A moment later, she saw his face peer at her from the doorway. "All right. All right. I'm going, you lunatic," she muttered, pushing herself up from the dusty road.

She decided not to ask the intense man where the brewery was and instead hobbled towards the town square, looking for familiar landmarks. A tall spire topped with a silver globe reflected a massive black cloud hovering nearby. And just then, the skies cracked open with a flood of rain. Pelted with large drops, August continued along the street, a bloody stream trailing behind her.

SIX

AUGUST

This time, August appeared soaking wet at Margaret's, shivering in the mist left by the rainstorm. "Oh, ya poor lass," said Margaret to the defeated woman standing in her doorway. "Get in here and sit yaself by the fire. Quickly!"

A fire burned in the middle of the cottage, smoke circling around a hole in the thatched roof, final spits of rain sizzling in the flames. Margaret guided August to a bench near the blaze. *Not super safe*, thought August, harnessing her judgement, hoping it would hold back the tears that lapped behind her eyes. It didn't work. August dropped her head to her lap, and the heaving sobs began.

August blurted garbled phrases, while Margaret sat beside her, softly rubbing her back.

"Where am I?

"I want to go home!

"Ripley will think I abandoned her.

"She needs her mother!

"Fuck! We need to close the deal!

"I miss Ripley.

"I miss Andrew.

"What is going on?"

Margaret sat patiently with August, rubbing slow concentric circles of calm. Eventually August's breath caught up to her body, and her nervous system relaxed. A tingle ran across her feet on the floor. With her tears finally exhausted, August sat up, a little warmer and a little softer. "Oh Jesus," August said as she wiped her eyes with her skirt.

"Is this Jesus a friend of yours?" asked Margaret.

August laughed softly. "Oh, you're funny, Margaret," she said, wiping her nose. "I'm so sorry to just show up here again and then endlessly cry. I don't normally do this to strangers."

"Well, ya aren't the first to puddle on my floor," she said with a kind smile, reaching for a pot of grasses beside the bench, her hair sparkling in the firelight.

August sighed and rubbed her face, as the flames flit around the logs. Hazel lay under the bed frame, the lavender eyes watching. "Now, August, I've heard many things here, like ya're a mother and under a heavy load. And I promise to keep them secret. But how about ya start with where ya're from?" said Margaret, her soft eyes peering around the grasses in her lap.

"Well, it's not here, wherever *here* is."

It was silent for a while, apart from the soft rhythm of Margaret weaving her long grasses. The warm cottage held a giant wooden shelf, which ran along an entire wall. Wooden boxes sat between folios of paper. The skull of a bat rested on a bundle of dried yellow flowers. A colourful and detailed illustration of mushrooms hung near the doorway;

at its edge August stared at a fungus draped with a delicate skirt of lace. Pulled back to the room, August looked straight into the fire, and asked deliberately, "Am I dead?"

It was Margaret's turn to chuckle. "Dead... I don't think it's quite my time, yet." She stopped weaving and looked at August. "Do ya feel dead?"

The ground was solid under her feet. The rain was wet on her body. Her breath filled and emptied her lungs. Everything was substantial and concrete. "No. I don't feel dead. If I was dead, I wouldn't be so bloody cold," said August with a smile.

"Fair that," said Margaret with a smile in return, and continued to weave.

"So, if I'm not dead, and this place isn't a hallucination, I've travelled through space and time?"

"I don't know about space, but ya don't sound from round here. What's ya village?"

"Victoria, BC."

"Near Lincolnshire?"

"No, It's not even on this continent."

"Not here at all..." said Margaret with a long pause.

"But I left from here, in Kent I mean. I was in Faversham at the brewery having a pint, and then I was bam – in mushrooms."

"And this *brewery*, is that a type of alehouse?"

"Yeah, I guess it is a kind of alehouse. It was called Shepherd Neame."

"We have nothing of that name except Louisa-Ray's, near the town square."

The grasses flowed easily as Margaret bent and wove each reedy length; She ended her row and looked at August.

"Well, I'm not sure how ya wound up here, but if an alehouse is the last thing ya 'member, we'd best visit Louisa-Ray. But tomorrow, when ya've had rest."

A yawn leached from August's mouth, the stress of the day unraveling, a weary softness settling on her legs. "Now, let's get ya to bed. But first off with ya clothes. I've already seen ya birthing suit once today," she said with a curl of humour on her lips.

August smiled and untied the first of many straps on her skirt. A thread of sadness wrapped around her heart: her distance from Ripley. "Thank you, Margaret. For, well, everything."

Margaret packed her grasses into the pot by her feet. "Well, ya aren't the first lost one to show up here, and ya won't be the last. There's many ways a thread travels."

SEVEN
AUGUST

August watched as Margaret carefully unwound the bandage on the little girl's arm. They'd made a stop at the Browns' cottage on the way to the alehouse.

They sat on a bench outside. The toddler squished her mouth as the last piece of cloth peeled off the skin. "Ya did great, Frankie," said Margaret, smiling at the little girl. "Ya arm looks much healed. I can tell ya've rested."

The girl's cheeks puffed as she said, "I did, Margaret. Just like you said. Jimmy tried to chase me yesterday. I said, 'No, Margaret says I must rest.' He was a bit angry, but not for long."

Margaret gently patted the little girl's shoulder, saying, "Ya did well and no doubt Jimmy was annoyed, but he's always been fussy, even as a babe," and winked.

Margaret dipped her fingers into a paste in a small clay pot, and gently dabbed the burn on the girl's forearm. August grimaced with misery; she couldn't touch her daughter, their distance increased every day.

From her basket, Margaret took a clean bandage and carefully wound it along the soothed burn.

"Margaret?" asked the little girl tentatively.

"Yah," Margaret replied, wrapping the arm.

"Do you have children?"

Margaret paused, then carried on winding the bandage, her fingers less assured. "No child of my own body, Frankie. But I've had the gift of many, many children." Her face softened. "I remember how ya came out cooing. I held ya as the sun rose and Ma rested. Ya gave me such great joy with ya soft coos."

A memory of August's two-day labor with Ripley rose. Her great fatigue, her plan to have a soothing home water birth that ended in the loud, bright white hospital. August watched her blood pool under the birthing table, her midwife pleading, "You *have* to tell your body to stop bleeding." *Add to the list: Order more Joni pads for perimenopause emergencies.* Margaret gave the girl a kiss on the forehead. "Ya have our permission to play all ya want. Resting is over."

The girl rose from her seat and wrapped her arms around Margaret's waist, head resting on the woman's bosom. "I love you, Margaret," Frankie said, squeezing the soft ripples of Margaret's shirt, then suddenly let go and bounced away, calling for Jimmy.

My heart might burst. The pain was so intense August was dizzy. A warm arm touched her. Margaret clutched August, a soothing overcame her tightness. "Ya miss ya own wee one, Ripley, is it?" asked Margaret softly in August's ear. Margaret smelt of rich earth, salt, and grasses.

"Yes," squeaked out August, her throat constricted.

They stood there, embracing each other, offering each body deep care, until August felt less alone.

"And here we are at Louisa-Ray's," said Margaret as they walked through a large open door. August's stomach fluttered as she entered through the intricately carved doorway. A large full moon at the top of the door shone on various animals, crows, a badger, a mouse, and forest fungi.

Long wooden tables with benches filled the space, smelling of ale and humans. At the rear of the large room a hallway reached back, piled with buckets and baskets. At three of the eight long tables, people gathered, some chatting, some in silence. August frowned, her eyes searching for something, anything familiar.

"Bevan," Margaret called out to a small boy carrying three giant mugs in his tiny arms. He placed them on a table next to a group of men and turned to them.

"Hello, Margaret. Here to see Louisa-Ray and Grace?"

"Aye and thanks," replied Margaret as the boy efficiently headed down the hallway.

A young woman, a girl really, about eighteen, came along the hallway and gave Margaret a great big hug. Her long red hair fell over her shoulders to her waist. "Oh, ya look well, Louisa-Ray," said Margaret. "Getting any sleep these nights?"

"Not too many complaints. Grace feeds like a starving ewe, so I've only to point this boob at her and she settles," said Louisa-Ray in a light Scottish lilt. "What can I do to help ya, Margaret?"

"This is August. She's trying to find her husband. Was she here two nights ago? Do ya remember?"

"Two nights ago," said Louisa-Ray as she looked at August's face. "I'd remember ya beautiful raven hair, but sorry, I don't recall ya or ya man. Are ya sure it was this alehouse?" she said, grabbing a cloth from her waistband and quickly wiping the tabletop. "'Tis another alehouse down the road at Whitstable that looks similar. Perhaps 'twas there? Sounds like ya had a very merry time if ya can't remember," she said with a chuckle and winked at August, putting the cloth back into her waistband.

August said sadly, looking into Louisa-Ray's green eyes, "Yeah, I don't think it was this pub."

"Pub, that's a funny word," said Louisa-Ray.

"You know, like 'public house'?" said August, conjuring a weak smile, determined not to look as depressed as she felt.

"Well, we are open to the public all right, sometimes for too many of the public, I might add," she tilted her head to one side and looked right into August's eyes. "If ya had been here, I'd remember that lovely smile."

August's cheeks reddened. *Great, I'm going to have a lesbian affair in this weird world.* She heard a small cry, and her mothering body tingled at a baby's hungry sounds.

Louisa-Ray reached her arm around her back and softly pat a bundle. "There you go, lass," Louisa-Ray said in a soft voice, then looked at the two women. "Well, sorry, I cannae be more help. I've got to get on. The women arrive soon with their surplus ale and it gets right busy with trading," she added with a smile, "but mostly they're busy with gossip."

Margaret and Louisa-Ray kissed each other on the cheek. August went numb to the alehouse mutters, the sour smell of wheat and barley; the hum of this world slipped away. *This is definitely not where I'm from... What the fuck am I supposed to do now?*

EIGHT
AUGUST

For the last three days, August hadn't left her bed. She'd sobbed or slept as Margaret continued her daily routine and services. Several times, August threw a blanket over herself when a villager visited; they'd come for herbal medicine, curious to glimpse the tall woman who talked oddly.

This morning Margaret forced August up. "I know ya're sad, but it's time for ya to get some air, August."

With frequent sighs, August belligerently dressed and followed Margaret into the woods.

August desperately wanted to sit and rest, but Margaret moved in slow but thoughtful steps, her green apron swishing back and forth. "Oh ya beauty, thank ya, Mother," said Margaret as she stopped and grasped the top of a small grey mushroom, her fingers gently twisting off the cap. She held the fungi towards the morning light piercing the forest canopy. "Luv, this will help with the pounding headache I suspect ya have," she said as she turned to August.

August checked in with her body. *I do have a headache, and I am fucking miserable. Where is my coffee! Add to the list: Replace the full caffeine coffee with half caff.*

Unable to reconcile this bizarre place with her home world, and suffering a blinding headache, August put the cap in her mouth. It tasted smoky and surprisingly chalky. The ache dulled as August's senses woke, a milky residue coating her mouth. The ground was soft beneath her feet, spongy with moss. A bird sang a gentle morning lullaby to wake the emerging ferns.

August watched the gentle woman place her hand against a fallen oak, touching the blanket of moss. Her other hand rested on her belt, near her knife. "Why don't you use your knife to slice the mushrooms?"

"August luv, fungi are much richer than their caps and stems." Margaret pushed aside a clump of bluebells, and a cluster of deep red mushrooms peeped out. "The root of each stem connects to the Mother. Uncountable ground pathways bind all that lives to water and to nourishment. By taking only the cap, we leave their roots intact and their connections open. We must protect the Mother, as they protects us all... Also, the fungi return more quickly if we don't slice them," she said practically.

"I think those are the mushrooms I found when I woke up," said August, bending down to view the wide red fungi.

"Ya're right. These are cosmos fungi, the very same ya rolled about in."

"So they grow here in the forest, but also in those logs. What's the deal with the massive fields of timbers?" asked August, her curiosity outweighing her melancholy for a moment.

Margaret sighed. With a stiff hip, she sat down on the fallen oak and stretched her legs. Margaret continued, "Those great fields are run by the sporelock guild. They're the ones who grow the cosmos. Ya mix the pulp of the fungi with hay and manure, then shape and cure the sporelock. It makes a sturdy material we use for building." Margaret paused. "I made my cottage from sporelock many years ago when I first arrived. But these days, it's only the guild that can make 'em."

"So this guild has a monopoly?"

"Aye. They run the fields and own the supplies we all need to build, but that's not the worst of it... their fields kill all."

"They kill the animals who live there?"

Margaret shifted her hip. "More than that. Fungi need balance. They live in small, family clusters, many in rings. In this way, they support their community. But clusters is not what the guild wants." Margaret pressed her hands on the small of her back and looked at the sky. "To grow cosmos in such mass upon the logs, the guild purifies the land first. Every field mouse, fly, and pheasant driven from the woods. Then they burn each branch, bush, and buttercup. At the end, the hands of the Divine Sphere sprinkle the soil with their purification, crushed walnut shells."

"Walnuts?"

"Their shells are a poison, kills all living things above

and beneath the soil. It's why nothing ever grows under the boughs of a mighty walnut."

"Huh," said August, thinking the field she'd woken in was actually a type of industrial site. Suddenly she exclaimed, "Did I get poisoned being naked there? Oh Jesus!"

"Oh no, August." Margaret said gently, tapping August's leg with her hand. "That field was purified some ten years ago. Ya're fine."

"Oh good," said August. Her heart slowed and then sped up again as something brushed against her leg.

Margaret smiled. "Well, hello there, Hazel. I wondered when ya'd join us."

Hazel brushed her head against August's calf. Calm flooded her body as August reached down to pet the cat. *I guess we're becoming friends.* After a couple of strokes, Hazel trotted over to Margaret. She hopped onto Margaret's lap, circled around the apron until she found the perfect spot to nestle between Margaret's legs. "There ya go, Hazel, have a rest, my friend," Margaret said as she rubbed the cat between her ears.

Hazel shut her eyes, and Margaret smiled. August watched them breathe in unison, like a mother and child as she sank to the ground. She saw Ripley: her little rainbow Wellington boots splashing in puddles on their forest walks; Ripley's brown eyes, so similar to her own, reflected in the water; Ripley's laugh as she danced in her pink leotard, smeared with chocolate stains and washable paint.

August shut her eyes, forcing her tears to stop. In the quiet, she heard Margaret's soft hum, a wood pigeon's coo,

Hazel's contented purr, her own breath matched with the frantic beat of her heart.

She knew this hallucination was real. The entire world made sense, in its own weird way. The fungal products, the villagers, even Louisa-Ray and baby Grace. Her rapidly beating heart reminded her of one thing: She was here, and her family wasn't.

NINE
AUGUST

In the west field of cosmos August stretched her arms in the air, and the tension in her upper back eased. *Add to the list: Do more thoracic yoga.* A wave of anxiety struck: the deal unfinished; her daughter crying, asking for her; the business slipping away. *Fuck!*

Margaret had encouraged, *forced*, her to find a routine. "Ya just cannae lay each day, August. The mind and ya bones needs movement, or else ya get stuck."

She was stuck. Stuck in a place with different strands of life, yet something here held on to her, clutched her tight to their patchwork world.

The dull ring of the lunch bell broke her thoughts. August weaved through the logs of cosmos not ready for harvest: the red stems too small, the mushroom heads the size of an orange.

At the pickers' station, August poured the cosmos she'd collected from her apron pocket into her assigned wicker basket. Small tendrils of red fungi, like hairs, clung to the inside of her pocket. She carefully added these straggling threads, anything to boost her load.

A sigh passed her lips as she watched her pickings rise two inches; August faced a scorching afternoon of harvest to reach the black line around the rim of her basket.

From behind, she heard Louisa-Ray's cheery voice, "All right there, August lass?"

"Yeah, right you are Louisa-Ray," said August, standing tall, bracing her hands against her lower back. "Just a bit sore."

"You've only been in these here fields a week. By the end of this moon ya'll be used to it all."

A week! Fuck, that means I've been here... almost fifteen days!

"Are ya sure ya's okay, August? Ya look mighty worried." She dropped her voice gently. "Ya know ya can tell me whatever 'tis on ya mind."

August bit back the tsunami of words, pursed her lips. "Ahhhh," said Louisa-Ray, "ya be sore because of the coming full moon. Did Margaret not give ya her tea? 'Tis so good for aches of the blooding."

August clued in. "Yes... that's right, my period is bugging me."

"Peer-e-odd: 'tis a funny word. But ya not wrong, the blooding comes with blues and pain and many odd things. Anyways, I just left the ale for ya lunch. And here's the gossip: Hugh Mandlestone, the lordship himself, may pass by. He's coming to the purification up the way. So keep ya eyes peeled – he's handsome, if gruff." She gave August a kiss on the cheek, and continued, "Now, take care of yaself, lass," and bustled off towards the foreman.

AUGUST

After lunch, the harvesters performed their orchestrated psilocybin stoop: bend, slice, pocket. "You want the cap to be the size of a newborn's skull," said the foreman, Wilf.

August fingered the small veins that wound across the fungi's cap. With every swipe of her blade, a rich umami tickled her nose. "He's here," came the awed voice of the young boy beside her.

August stood up, shielding her eyes with her hand, and looked towards the track beside the field. High on a muscular white horse sat a middle-aged man with a weathered face, hair streaked with silver like mycelium threading through dark soil. *Hugh, I guess. Definitely giving me guildmaster energy.*

Hugh paced his strong steed along the fence, a subtle assurance in his stride, his angular face and green eyes searching. Four young men in cream capes waited in stillness for their master to complete his assessment. Wilf took the sweaty brown hat from his head and bowed deeply to the visitors. With one strong hand appearing from his cape Hugh gave a sharp tug on the reins and pulled his horse back to the track. The sporelock crest fixed to the capes glittered, the silver embroidery catching the low afternoon sun. Cream wraps swayed as the young men turned to follow, their sporelock crests moved in unison, as their feet stamped the earth.

"Right, back to work," yelled Wilf, placing his hat on his head.

"They say this full moon he'll *finally* have a son," muttered the boy, placing his knife on a cosmos, slicing its stem.

August cut through a tender stem, the knife heavy in her hand, every swipe of her blade a betrayal. A betrayal to Margaret and the Mother. A betrayal to her old life. The tears of everything she'd lost slipped down her face, sending an ancient story of grief to the ground beneath her feet.

TEN
AUGUST

August sat alone outside the cottage, her back aching. The vast stars deepened as August stared; small dots connected galactic webs in the sky, mirroring the linked world beneath her feet. August shifted her ankles, earth coating her toes, sticking to her nails. *I can't even see the Milky Way.*

August knew she wasn't hallucinating. This world was too specific: the transparent gall fungi that clung to the edges of rocks and floated in the water like tiny glass pompoms.

Bats zipped in the blue light, catching dinner in the darkening forest. She took a deep breath; the soft zips relaxing her muscles. *This land seems so unreal and yet somehow I also feel so connected.*

August already intuited love and care from the women here. What surprised her was the link she observed each morning when she rose from her bed, like the land wanted her here. The chilly hand of guilt rose from her stomach and sent pulses through her body, vibrations that wouldn't stop, only increased in power. Instinctively, August stood and screamed, "ARGGHHHH."

As the long scream left her body, the rage, grief, disappointment, and fear depleted every single cell. She sensed a response; a wave of energy rose through her bare feet and travelled through the threads of her body.

Startled, August touched her throat, the skin thick with loneliness. She placed her hand on her heart. The vacant hollow under her palm missed Ripley's tender kiss, Tabatha's laugh that made them both shake with joy, Andrew's determination to bring stability and security to their family.

Soft light stretched through the galaxy above her, casting a shadow of August's body on the ground. Two Augusts, two women trapped in the light and the dark.

Suddenly, she gripped the earth with her toes. "I am going to get home," she whispered to the stars.

August refused to accept she was stuck. Her body tingled with power, her voice strengthened as she thrust her arms in the air. "I'm going to do *everything* I can to get home. Ripley, I'm coming!"

Determination grew in her mind to reach her daughter, close the floundering deal, and make peace with Andrew. She knew the Doctor would not pop out of the blue box and whisk her home. It would be her strength, grit, and smarts that would build her bridge back, *plus a good dose of ale! Create new to do list: get home.*

August spent the rest of the night weaving her plan and wondering how these webbed worlds were connected.

ELEVEN
MARGARET

Margaret heard a tipsy August singing as she tottered to the cottage. *Another night of ale excess.* Even through the cottage door, Margaret could hear August's low voice tangled with a sparrow's, the bird sending its last message for the day.

This evening August's song held a refrain, "Let it be." The word "wisdom" echoed in their mind. The wisdom they'd learnt from this natural world. This place that helped them heal, counsel, and care for all. Their right hip ached in its familiar pattern, a reminder of time, they all aged like the Mother trees. *I must pass this wisdom on.*

August approached the cottage, her voice high, and stopped mid-phrase. A pause, and August continued, "Hear that Hazel?... You have words of wisdom, cat!"

Margaret chuckled. *Hazel has many words of wisdom, wisdom of ancient generations.*

There was a thump, then a scrape at the door. "Margaret... oh, Margaret," came August's singsong voice mimicking Old English, "I need help to open the door, me lady."

Margaret put their mortar and pestle on the bench, wiped their hands on their apron. They tried to push the door open, but it wouldn't shift.

"Who's touching my butt?" giggled August through the door.

"Move ya'self out of the way," called Margaret, slightly annoyed. *It seems she will never tire of this ale "experiment," as she calls it. And with the Kentish Cup coming, more ale will flow. She'll be in a right state then.*

"Fine," yelled August and, after a few scuffing sounds, the door gave enough inches so she could squeeze through the gap on hands and knees.

Inside, August sat on the ground, knees dusty, swaying slightly, and pointed at Margaret. "It's not bloody working!" she hiccupped and spoke at the same time.

Margaret sat slowly down next to her, pushing the knife in the belt of their apron to the side. "What's not working?" they asked calmly.

"I can't get home to my family, Margaret. This was supposed to work. I was going to take one sip of every ale and find the magical brew that sent me here to send me home, but I've tried them *all*," August said with a small burp. "I'm *still* stuck in this world of fungi. My back is fucking sore from all the bending. I don't even notice that smell anymore... I miss Ripley... she'll think I've abandoned her! I'm not even supposed to be *here*," said August, the word "here" more like a shriek. With a sharp jolt, Margaret's own grief of abandonment flickered in their stomach.

Margaret had also never known their parents. One spring morning, Purity Sister Penelope, an attendant for the

Divine Sphere, found a baby in their walled walnut orchard. As Penelope searched the rough blanket for a note or clue, the sister gasped and covered her lips as she studied a baby with both sex organs.

With a deep breath, Margaret came back to the present. "I know ya feel out of place, August. I know ya aren't where ya want to be," sympathized Margaret.

"You can see it. I can see it. So why can't God, or the devil, or the Mother or whoever the fuck did this send me home? I want to go home. I need to see Ripley and save my b-b-business," August barely got the words out when she retched.

Two more retches and August vomited a smattering of ale onto the cottage floor. *This woman who doesn't fit can't settle but she also can't leave. I know that all too well.*

Even as a baby Margaret's unsettledness followed them like a shadow through the walnut orchard and its halls. The Purity Sisters hired a wet nurse from the local jewellery guild, but the large-breasted woman refused to feed the baby because of its "impure body." In quiet speed, the wet nurse left the orchard with a purse of expensive purity walnuts.

The sisters raised the dual sex baby as a girl and named them Margaret. The thick red orchard walls kept out much of the whispers and shame that waited on the outside, but nothing could unpick the abandonment woven deeply through their soul.

August looked at Margaret, embarrassment rising in her eyes. "Oh Christ, I'm so sorry, Margaret. You must be sick of my drunken wretchedness," she said, wiping her lips with her skirt.

"It's true. Ya be a wretch," said Margaret in a deadpan tone, and then smirked as they got up with from the floor and grabbed a broom. Margaret knew the woman was struggling: her excessive drinking, her odd songs and fiddlesome words. *They certainly aren't of this world. I wonder what wisdom she carries.* But it wasn't for them to say; it was their nature, and their work, to keep secrets.

August smiled. "Oh, and I forgot you're also funny." She took a deep breath and sighed out, "I don't know what to do... "

"Well, perhaps the ale is not the way back to ya home?"

"I guess not," said August sagging on the floor, "but I have no idea what to try next."

"I've a couple ideas for that."

"You do?" August asked, perking up a little.

"Ya, but we'll tend on that tomorrow. Right now, let's get ya to bed," said Margaret, as they put the broom, along with the pile of sick, by the front door. Margaret put their arm out to August, "Come on, luv, take comfort in ya bed."

August reached for Margaret's hand and smiled contentedly as Margaret tucked her into bed.

With August snoring, Margaret called for Hazel. They took off their socks, then pressed their toes into the earthen floor. Margaret brought the dark black cat to mind, her blazing purple eyes and said in thought, *Hazel, come to me.*

Two minutes later, a shining grey nose pushed the

cottage door open, a black body oozing into the room, hopping onto Margaret's lap.

Margaret stroked Hazel from tip to tail in slow, steady pets. The cat rubbed her cheek against their hand, then placed her right paw on Margaret's wrist; their connection was made. In their mind, Margaret spoke to the Mother Network.

Mother, I'm worried. My sister Carers are being taken in greater numbers. All this ancient knowledge we carry, I worry it will be lost.

We agree, Margaret, came the voice of the network, carried into Margaret's mind by Hazel.

What can I do?

We have been planning for this. We will reveal all soon.

But what of this strange woman in my care...

Hazel removed her paw from Margaret's wrist, the question cut off. The cat gave them a slow blink, then bolted from their lap and out of the cottage into the dark.

Margaret sighed and closed their eyes. *I hear August snoring. I hear the wind tickling the leaves. I feel the connected earth under my feet. I am settled, even in such uncertainty.*

Margaret always searched for contentment. Even as their body unfurled during puberty, they recognized the strength of having all sexes. They saw their body and mind as another organism, like the fungi, another who understood a world beyond the binary. But it was only the Mother Network who knew their secret, not even their sister Thread Carers knew of their shame. No one would see the real them.

Margaret detected a rush of warm energy from deep

beneath their feet. They breathed in their own love, flushed their pained past from their mind, and settled into a moment of connectedness with the many threaded webs of the universe. And they wondered if August perceived a connection to the Mother as well.

TWELVE
AUGUST

"Oh, lass, ya're too smart to be harvesting cosmos," said Louisa-Ray to August as Louisa-Ray sorted through a cluster of papers.

August, Margaret, and Louisa-Ray sat at the back of the inn. It was a slow Sunday afternoon with two greying men sipping ale in quiet conversation near the door. Louisa-Ray unwound the cloth tie from her hair, smoothed her long red waves with her fingers, and continued, "Picking fungi is a good enough job, but ya got smarts in that head there, lass. And Bethany told me they're looking for an accounts man up at the great house." Louisa-Ray wrapped her hair into a ponytail and secured a tight bun on her head.

"Accounts, like bookkeeping?" asked August.

"The same," said Louisa-Ray. "Just like all this nonsense here... Aha!" she exclaimed, finding the piece of paper she'd been hunting for and scribbling on it with a pencil.

August sipped the herbal tea Margaret had made. It was good for "the heat strikes" as Margaret called them. She took another sip. *Add to the new list: See what I can find at the great house.*

"There's much to do before the Herding. The Divine Sphere closes the half-yearly books at the running of the animals. I wouldn't be doing all this for naught. Oh, Mother, where is that paper from the cidery?" exclaimed an exasperated Louisa-Ray as she stood up. "It must be in the bloody storeroom," she said, annoyed, and headed to the back.

August rubbed her fingers against her cup of tea. Margaret seemed unusually quiet, almost pensive. August tentatively asked, "So, what exactly is this running of the animals? I've heard several people mention the Herding. Is it a livestock show?"

Margaret's eyes came into focus like she'd returned from elsewhere. "It is a show, of sorts, but I think it isn't what ya mean," said Margaret, sipping her tea. "When the River Elders flower, the blood moon appears. That's the one coming to us next week. This brings the Herding. We also have a second moon, in the dead of winter, the snow moon, when the animals come as well." Margaret took a deep breath. "At the Herding time, one animal from our lands, and airs, rises to stampede across the soil. 'Tis like a giant rug thrown over everything. The animals rush as if driven by a burning we cannae see. Stories have always existed of the Herding, but the first ever told to us was of the rats. Thousands of rats swept from the east through the fields and towns, nibbling on crops, attacking babies, munching anything in their path. We've come to learn, and raise ourselves in towers when the Herding comes."

August pinched her mouth, skepticism crept into her

voice, "You're telling me twice a year a single animal gets together with all its buddies and races across the country?"

Margaret gave a small chuckle. "It does sound daft, I know. But it has its danger. Folks are injured and even killed."

"What?" August butted in. "People have died?"

"It is hard to believe if ya've never seen it," said Margaret.

The two women sat in silence. Margaret traced a circle on the table with her finger, over and over. *Really, a giant herd of animals that kill people? This is whacked*, thought August, considering the potential for death and the breadth of animals that might herd. "What were the animals in your first Herding?"

"Ah, it was the wolves," answered Margaret, her eyes twinkling. "They came running from the east, galloping along streams, raiding the land."

"Sweet Jesus, wolves," exclaimed August. "That's way more dangerous than rats!"

"At the time, I lived in the walnut orchard, so it was easy for me to barricade myself. I peeked from a hole in the shutter and watched the snarling mass roll across the lands. And the next day I got a close look."

"What did you see?" asked August, catching Margaret's excitement.

"The next morning Sister Beatrice snuck us from the walled orchard. She took every moment to teach us the ways of the land. We came upon a dead wolf lying on its side beside the stream. Beatrice wouldn't let us get close, so we sat nearby. She told us to wait. Slowly, the wolf shrunk; it was as if the air and the blood and the bone were sucked into the earth. All that was left was a cluster of light blue cups, fungi we'd never eyed before. They were the size of a mug, the blue of a robin's egg, with a thick golden band around the rim."

"Whoa. Do the animals always leave behind mushrooms?"

"They do, and they're a deadly sort if taken by mouth."

"So, after the Herding, they leave a bunch of poisonous mushrooms?"

"Not for long, August. After each Herding we gather the cups. For centuries, we'd taken them back to the forest, gifted them back to the land. But these days the Divine Sphere takes the gold caps," Margaret swallowed, "and they burn them."

"Why?"

"The Divine Sphere believes the Herding and the cups are punishment from their god, the Lord of Purity. Their tales say the Lord sends the Herding so everyone can purify ourselves."

"But you don't believe that, you believe in the Mother and – "

"Shh, August," said Margaret, cutting her off, panic in her eyes. Quietly she continued, "Ya must be careful out here. Our cottage is safe, but here, ya must be wise with ya words."

"What are ya two lasses whispering about?" called Louisa-Ray, as she returned with a tray of food and mugs. "I'm done with all me ridiculous papers. And since 'tis quiet and wee Grace is a little from waking, let's relax."

AUGUST

Sometime later, the women had finished the salted cod, pickled onions, cheese, and bread. Grace sat on Margaret's lap, periodically grabbing for the cheese knife with her pudgy hands, bread crumbs around her mouth.

"So," said August slowly, "if I wanted to get the accounts position at the great house, do I have an interview?"

"Have a what view?" asked Louisa-Ray, looking at Margaret.

August blushed as Margaret replied, "I think she means a placement."

"Oh, right. Well, placement is easy, August. Ya go straight to them kitchens around the back of the house and ask for our Bethany. I'll get word to her that ya're comin' and she'll take ya straight to Angus, the head of the house. Angus is an all right sort, a bit cranky, but he works hard to support lovely Maggie. But those bloody girls of his are useless. If they were my girls..."

"Got it," said August. "Go to the house, ask for Bethany, and speak to Angus. Plus his girls are bloody useless. Seems straightforward. Do I need to bring anything?"

Louisa-Ray laughed, "Like what, bring a cow to milk?"

August added, "I just mean..."

"Och, August, I'm just razzing ya," said Louisa-Ray, laughing as she took Grace from Margaret's outstretched arms as the woman stood up.

"I must be off," said Margaret. "I promised Francis I'd look in and see to his foot before bed."

"'Tis late for that," said Louisa-Ray.

"'Tis," said Margaret quickly, "but that is as it is." She kissed Grace on the forehead, the light blue eyes lovingly blinked back at her. With a squeeze on Louisa-Ray's and August's shoulders, Margaret left the inn, clanging the front door behind her.

"Is Margaret, all right these days?" asked Louisa-Ray.

"I think so. Why?"

"She was quiet tonight and looks more tired than usual. Ah, 'tis probably naught," said Louisa-Ray as she took a final sip from her mug.

Grace was a magnet who held August's eyes fast. Those cupped cheeks, those long eyelashes. *Oh, Ripley.* "Well, this wee bairn needs her proper rest. I'm to take her for a walk before. Care to come along?" asked Louisa-Ray.

***

THE STARS ARRIVED AS THE TWO WOMEN WALKED the tracks by the sporelock fields. Grace slept, her right arm hanging from the cloth sling, her face pressed into Louisa-Ray's back, eyes closed – a contentedness only babies know. Louisa-Ray bumped her shoulder against August's and softly said, "Ya know, we're well pleased ya came to us."

A terrible tension ached in August's chest. "Well, I'm glad to have met you and Grace as well. And of course Margaret... I wouldn't be here without her."

"Ya're right there. Margaret is absolutely the wisest

woman I well know," said Louisa-Ray. "She gave me the strength I needed when this wee one was born."

Louisa-Ray stopped walking. "'Tis important we watch out for her," she said seriously.

"Of course," replied August. "But why… "

"The Divine Sphere is looking for women of her kind, those with knowledge of the Mother Network. I hate to think what might happen if… Oh Mother, I just cannae bear it."

"Is it really that serious?" August's heart began beating more quickly.

"Oh, aye, deathly serious. Across our county they're taking women most weeks. The stories I hear tell at the inn… I dare not share them with Margaret. I don't want her to worry so."

August grabbed Louisa-Ray's hand. "I promise I'll do anything I can to protect Margaret."

Louisa-Ray gave a soft smile. "I reckon ya will. Many thanks."

The duo continued walking hand in hand, and August wondered how much danger Margaret might really be in.

THIRTEEN
MARGARET

Margaret awoke to the chirping of sparrows. They sat up slowly, the weight of their years on their hips, and smiled. *Another beautiful day. Thank you, Mother.*

They puttered around the cottage, following a pattern weaved over the years: Stoke the fire, put on the kettle, fetch more wood for midmorning, then walk to rinse their face in the cool stream. At the water's edge, silver ribbons curled in the water. Then, with their bucket of water, Margaret walked the well-worn path to the cottage, their empty fingers tickling the silver-tipped foxgloves.

Margaret poured boiling water over fennel seeds, then took their mug of tea outside. In their sacred morning seat, Margaret focussed their mind. August was already away to the cosmos fields for a day of picking, a small jar of comfrey paste in her apron to ease her back. Margaret sipped their tea, warm and spicy in their mouth.

Thoughts crashed and floundered in their mind. This morning's practice was not so calm. The pain August carried so heavily fed the shame of their own abandonment. The roots of loneliness grew through their body, to spread and suffocate their mind. They took a deep breath, closed their eyes, and focussed on the ground beneath their feet.

Their mind settled, but sparked again. This time, it burst with anxiousness: more Carers being taken, a restlessness in the Mother they'd never noticed before. *How can I support you, Mother? How do I protect my sisters? I fear I run out of time.*

Margaret sipped their tea and sat with their feelings: the worry that their knowledge could be lost, rich collective wisdom gone, expertise not there for the women who would come. Their curious need to help August get back home, to her other life and family. Both threads ran through their body, gushing like a current. They took a breath.

Large, fluffy bees buzzed along the cusp of a comfrey bloom. With their feet on the earth and the sun on their face, Margaret sat still and watched. *I see and hear you all.*

"Hello? Margaret?" came a deep voice from the meadow.

Margaret stood from the bench to see Hugh's weathered face traipsing through the grasses, his sporelock cape over his shoulder like a sash. His eyes flicked around, always on the lookout. "Hugh, welcome," said Margaret warmly and waved their arm.

Seated beside Margaret, Hugh cupped his one large, rough hand around his tea. His muscular arms rested on his thighs, his crushed hand draped over his knee. His boot buckles shone in the morning light.

"Ya're soon to be a father," said Margaret.

"Yes," said Hugh, and sipped his tea. "And that's part of why I'm here." He ground his right boot into the soil, a nervous tick he'd had since his birth.

Margaret sipped their tea and waited.

"The Sphere demand I have a maister at the birth, and only a maister."

"We thought that might be."

Hugh shifted his arms, his voice cracked, "The last time was so... "

"I know," said Margaret, gently putting their hand on his. "Ya both wanted the babe so much, but the poor little one was too early. It wasn't ya fault. Send Yvonne to me this week and I'll take a look, especially as she's thick with two." They patted Hugh's arm gently.

"Many thanks," he said, looking at the meadow.

A small deer popped from the forest, peering into the grassland. "Ya're back," Margaret called to the fawn. "She thinks she'll find a way into the bounty," said Margaret with a chuckle, gesturing to the fenced garden.

"I doubt there's a deer in these woods that could get through your tight weaves, Margaret."

"I reckon ya lovely father, Thomas's, were stronger."

Margaret waited for Hugh to speak. His lips opened

and rapidly shut, a man trying to stop many things from coming out.

Hugh sighed. "He was good with a bind."

"He sure was, and such a fast study of fungi. I never knew another who took to it quite like Thomas."

Hugh smiled. "Those afternoons in the forest with him, foraging, sketching, talking… They're the best moments we had."

"I'm glad of it, Hugh. Ya father loved ya, but suffered so deeply from the despair."

The fawn, who'd been circling the garden, found a stalk of tansy bursting over the fence. With a swipe of her tongue, she cleared the branch of its leaves, leaving behind a barren twig. "She got one," said Margaret as a wave passed over Hugh's face, the same waves she'd watched Thomas struggle with. "Speaking of the despair, do ya – "

Hugh cut Margaret off. "I must get back to the house," he said as he rose, handing Margaret the cup, startling the fawn, who bounded back to the safety of the forest. "Thank you for the tea and for helping Yvonne. And, Margaret," he said, a serious tone in his voice, "be careful. The Sphere is excitable, especially with the new text circulating. The word 'Wikka' is on everyone's lips." Hugh reached for Margaret's shoulder. "Just watch yourself with the Sphere… Please."

Margaret patted his hand. "I will, and thank you for the warning, Hugh."

Hugh quickly pulled his arm away and grabbed his cape from the bench. With a nod, he flung his cream clothing over his shoulder, his boots clomping in the grasses as he walked to the forest.

Margaret watched Hugh rock side to side. He'd walked

in a sideways motion even as a boy. The day they tended his crushed hand he'd been eighteen. He sat so scarily still as they moved his finger bones for blood flow. For a moment, Margaret worried Hugh's calm would flow into despair. That he might follow the path of his father and take to bed for weeks. They'd worried he'd never rise, or worse.

Margaret sipped the last of their tea. The young man had been fine and adjusted to his new hand. He let nothing stop his growing sporelock trade. *He's a man who battles much. I hope he has enough strength in reserve for whatever Mother believes is coming.*

FOURTEEN
AUGUST

"I don't want to go to the House of the Divine Sphere," said August. *I sound like a petulant child, but the more I learn about this "Divine Sphere," the more I'm convinced Tom Cruise will show up.*

Margaret and August were almost at the top of a rise, walking a single line along a trodden path. August couldn't stop staring at the boots on Margaret's feet: knee-high boots made of groundskin, leather-like fabric created from pressed waterproof fungi. The thick covering trapped Margaret's feet like shackles. "August, we all must go to the House of the Divine Sphere, and today 'tis time for ya to be protected, for ya to get ya boots," said Margaret in an oddly demure voice.

August's eyes quickly dropped to the groundskin boots constricting Margaret's feet.

"My own boots? Why do I need my own boots? You don't even really wear yours," said August, eyeing the thick silver buckles.

Margaret softened her voice, "The Divine Sphere knows many can draw power through our feet, so they block it with metal plates stitched into the soles."

"That's outrageous! I am not – " said August, quickly cut off by Margaret.

"August," said Margaret firmly, turning to face her. She glanced at the young couple following them up the hill and whispered, "Look, we get that ya do not want to go and ya do not want boots. But we have to go and we have to obey. The work we do in community is important; the mas, the babes, the elders – they all need us. To disobey the Divine Sphere would put them all at risk. We will not do that."

August nodded as she considered Margaret's role: a counsellor, midwife, healer, and friend to everyone. Even the fungi depended on her. "Okay, I get it. I'm sorry."

Margaret patted August on the shoulder and smiled a little. "'Tis okay. Let us keep going. We are almost there."

As the rise melted into the landscape, a silver metal dome rose from a cleared meadow below. "Oh my God. Is that the church?" August's eyes squinted.

"Ya, 'tis the house of the Divine Sphere."

Sunshine reflected off the silver dome, glaring in August's eyes. The only mark on the polished surface was a black hole near the horizon. Figures disappeared one at a time, like ants reaching their colony.

August followed Margaret down a dark hallway that opened inside the sphere. The same highly polished silver metal covered their heads and long metal ropes with clusters of round lights hung from the ceiling. Dots of light shimmered across every surface, the globe glowing from the inside. August vowed to pay close attention; anything here could be a clue to lead her home.

The metal amphitheatre had circular rows of benches that curved along the walls in concentric circles. They all faced the large circular stage, so that all eyes were directed forward.

Margaret awkwardly took several steps down, then turned left. August followed and took a seat as Margaret sat down. "When does the disco music begin?" whispered August. In return, Margaret gave an odd smile that quickly withered. August's right thigh jiggled and her palms wet slightly.

As she scanned the theatre, August saw Louisa-Ray feeding Grace, seated next to another woman she'd met once when she'd brought extra ale for sale. The sphere was full, not a seat empty.

A minor note sounded as a metal bell rang with slow, repetitive clangs. On the stage floor, a trapdoor slid open, revealing a set of stairs to a space beneath. A line of men wearing long white robes with detailed silver embroidery held a long chain with a brassy metal globe swinging from each end. The men rose from the stairwell, their buzz-cut heads bobbing as they stepped in time to the clang of the bell. When the sixth man appeared, the trapdoor slid shut, and the stage was a perfect circle again.

Grouped in pairs, the men walked in concentric circles, following round silver outlines on the floor. The circles, the men, and their swinging globes interlinked like a Venn diagram; the men moved with the clangs, weaving around each other. A wispy smoke flowed from the swaying globes; a smell like bleach, an acidic burning filled the air. Silence but for the shuffling of feet and the clang of the bell. With a final long ring, the men stopped in unison and placed their spheres on the ground, wrapping the chains like the coil of a snake.

August noticed a small section of ten silver seats, raised higher than everyone else. *There's Hugh. Those must be the other guild-masters.* Each man wore a large silver pendant around his neck, filled with a fabric shaded in grey or white. One woman sat beside each man, their heads bent to the floor, eyes turned down, the top of each head shimmering with jewels. August caught the eyes of Hugh, his left hand resting in his lap, peppery hair hanging over his brows, curious green eyes that held on her. She rapidly glanced away.

In the centre of the silver circles, a second trapdoor opened. A podium rose slowly, holding a much older man in a similar white robe with a crown of transparent gall fungi shimmering on his sheared head. He held a tall staff with a silver globe atop. The podium stopped and the elderly man spoke, his voice amplified by the theatre: "We, the brothers of the Divine Sphere, graciously serve the Lord of Purity.

"We seek to purify with his divine light.

"This light sheds us of our fungal sins and strips us of impurity.

"He is the one that brings light to the dark.

"Purification is the way of the Divine Sphere."

The audience's voices joined in unison, startling August: "Purification is the way of the Divine Sphere."

August noticed Margaret's lips moved, but she didn't think any words came out.

The man raised his globe staff and struck the plinth's metal floor, the sound reverberating. "Welcome, impure ones, to your October ceremony."

"We welcome you, Father Gerard," replied the audience.

"Today is indeed a special day for us. We have two members in desperate need of protection." August froze, her feet tingling. "Brothers, deliver the purity boots!"

The bell sounded again as two men in creamy robes walked around the sphere's top level. August's hands shook. Margaret held them gently and whispered, "Ya will be okay, August; just follow along."

One man in cream walked down the staircase behind them and stopped at the end of their row. He placed a tall pair of brown boots in the hands of the woman seated at the end. Father Gerard continued, "Puritans, raise your palms, honour the boots, and pass them along."

The woman with the boots in her palms lowered her forehead until it touched the boots' upper, her face resting against the smooth groundskin. She raised her head, then passed the boots to the young man on her left, who also placed his forehead against the boots. Down the row the boots continued, until the young girl sitting beside August placed them in August's palms; cold metal soles slipped against wet skin. August briefly touched eyes with her fellow designee, a young man across the sphere receiving his boots; August recognized the fear and embarrassment on his face.

Her body quivered as voices rose in unison. "You will be protected by the Lord of Light. He will walk you from the darkness into the light. Purification is the way of the Divine Sphere!"

Father Gerard banged his staff a second time. "Now, let our brothers raise their voices to purify your minds."

The brothers in the concentric circles hummed a low song, a breathy harmony. "Love, put ya boots on," whispered Margaret, gently tapping August's leg, her face dimmed. August's shaky hands settled as she leant over her skirt and struggled to place her feet in the stiff boots. The groundskin was fresh and tough, the metal soles of the boots inflexible. August's breath slowed as the curious eyes left her, drawn to the harmonic humming from the stage. *Okay, that wasn't so bad. But these are the world's most uncomfortable boots. Add to the new list: See if these boots might help me get home.*

Settled in her seat, August saw a black metal box moving along each row. Villagers placed a single coin into a slit on the top. Eventually, the box came down their row and Margaret thrust a coin into August's palm. With the cold cube on her lap, August read the words "PURIFICATION FEE" in stamped capital letters. She dropped her coin. It rattled against the others in its new home.

August's mind flashed: a fluttering red cloak of a handmaid, a red rising phoenix stamped on a military helmet ready for space battle, thick red flames consuming banned books in a dark night. She gazed around the large amphitheatre, wondering who else resisted. Who else, like Margaret, believed fungi to be integral, an organic scale balancing the land?

August realized it was impossible to tell and let the rest of the ceremony wash over her, her mind more determined to help Margaret and Louisa-Ray bring balance to the land.

FIFTEEN
MARGARET

THE EARLY MORNING SUN CRESTED THE TIPS OF the great oaks and brought Margaret's figure into view, their body a soft watercolour against the land.

As soon as Margaret climbed the first hill, along the path from the village, they sat down to peel off their boots. They fumbled with the stiff buckle, their fingers swollen and whispered to themselves, *take the time you need. There is no rush.*

With a gasp, Margaret pulled one foot from their boot and then the other. They could breathe again, the invisible twine spun around their chest loosened. They took a deep breath in and let it out.

Margaret dug their toes into the soil and closed their eyes. The vibrations they sensed were pulsing quickly, different from their usual slow thumps. Their fear rose in a gush; they breathed again to slow it all down.

Then a soft brush of warm fur on their foot caused them to smile and open their eyes. Hazel sat at their feet, her dark fur tinged with a deep chestnut colour in the early morning light, cleaning her left paw. Her purple eyes were firmly fixed on a spot of fluff that needed an intense morning bath. Margaret reached down and pet Hazel's head with their sore fingers. "Hello, my love," they said.

Hazel stopped her cleaning, put her paw of interest down, and looked at Margaret, her purple irises stretching to the sides like a smile. Then Hazel picked up her paw again and took up her task.

Margaret stretched their legs out, enjoying the sensation of length along the back of their thighs after a busy night of sitting, leaning across the card table, and laughing with their friends.

They lay down on their back and watched the tops of the oak trees slip out of the night shadows and into flickers of sunshine. A robin carried a branch of hyssop in its mouth and they marvelled at the knowledge the mother bird possessed: hyssop to repel flea and lice from her nest and protect her young. *We carry so much. So much we've learnt from our many selves, our communities and our Mother Network.* The worry crept back, the burnings, the rising strength of the Divine Light, the nervousness they intuited from every Thread Carer across the network.

A soft weight grew on their chest as Hazel crouched down, her paws gently kneading against the fabric by Margaret's heart. "Oh, Hazel, you always know how to help."

As Margaret watched, the cat shut her eyes and dropped her chin to her furry chest, their connection made. And in their mind Margaret heard the Mother Network.

Margaret, we know how worried you are. We know how anxious you are. We know things are not in balance.

Yes, Mother, it feels unsettled.
We all sense the trouble and we'd like to ask for your help.
Of course, anything you need.

There was a pause and Margaret heard their soft breath in unison with Hazel's. Then the Mother Network spoke again.

We ask you to gather up all your knowledge and that of your sisters, then share it in two very specific ways.

Of course.

First, we need you to share your skills with another. Bethany has great instincts and a large capacity for caring. She will be the one who studies under your care.

Ah, Bethany is a good choice. I would be honoured to help her flourish.

The second ask is much greater. We need you to share your rich knowledge back into our network. And we wish it wasn't so, but this ritual will be exhausting. Each time you directly connect with us, your own body will deplete.

Hazel gently rose and fell as Margaret took a deep breath. They responded with their mind: *I understand. I vow to share all that I know, and the knowledge of my sisters. It is my privilege to contribute to the mentorship of the deceased.*

We thank you, Margaret. And when you are ready to begin the transfer, Hazel will guide you through the night ritual. We see you for who you are, Margaret, and we appreciate you.

A moment of great love, security, and peace fed Margaret, then the connection broke off.

Margaret opened their eyes and watched Hazel rise and stretch her front paws out towards their face, then delicately hop off and meander away through a clump of butter fungi, their small yellow nest full of butter-yellow fruit reaching out to the early morning sun.

There was a new power tingling in their mind and body. *I will do everything the Mother Network needs. The threads connect me to my past, my present, and my future.* A smile broke on their lips as the scent of thyme and butter fungi filled their nose and everything felt a little lighter.

SIXTEEN
AUGUST

THE WALK TO THE MANDLESTONE HOUSE WAS farther than August imagined. *Where was Margaret this morning?* she thought, stepping over patches of moss towards the looming building. August had risen to find Margaret's bed made and no water boiling on the fire. *I'll find out where she got to tonight*, she thought as her feet ached in her stiff, constricting boots.

She passed by travellers coming the other way. One man led a cart stuffed with noisy children who were smacking each other. The youngest picked his nose, wiped it on his short pants. The man leading his horse turned to the cart and yelled, "Would you shut down all the bother? Or I'll give you a bother!"

The noise subsided but slowly rose as someone got pinched, and another needed a pee. In a moment of relief from her all-consuming desire to get home, August reflected on her access to birth control, her choices over her body, her decision to have one child and not a gaggle. *One and done.* Young girls came to Margaret with trepidation in their movements, and each left with a round bag of herbs, a look of shame across their faces.

The red sporelock house did not welcome August as she stepped through the large silver gate. Cursive script screamed "Mandlestone," the title surrounded by overlapping concentric circles. *Well, this isn't* Bridgerton, *more like* Tess of the d'Urbervilles, thought August, the moisture clinging to the red walls, condensation thick on the windowpanes. August walked around the east side of the big house, as Louisa-Ray told her, to a well-worn door, and knocked. She waited a moment, noting a bucket of wet cloth waiting to be hung on a line, a pile of rotting turnips, and two mating pigeons by an oak tree.

She knocked again and watched the pigeons finish their afternoon delight. *I hope that was consensual.* And still nobody answered. She grabbed the big iron ring, twisted it, and pushed the door open.

The room was large, hot, and smokey. August instinctively put her hand to her nose. Someone in the haze shrieked by the giant fireplace and flapped at the billowing smoke with their apron. Two tween girls ran around a large wooden table, chasing each other. One held a long pink ribbon and kept flicking the other, who looked grumpy and sad, then laughed and gave chase, brushing past August as they ran outside. A small spotted dog rested with ease at the foot of the table.

Masses of smoke billowed from the fireplace and, through the murk, August could make out two women. They pushed long sticks into the smoke and up the chimney. The shorter one hopped on a chair and, on the tip of her toes, reached inside the fireplace with a long stick. Bang.

Bang. Bang. Followed by a gush of soot that consumed the room.

August brushed soot from her face, dark waves danced, blackness touching every surface. Harmonious coughing fits from everyone sent the dog fleeing. "Great firestones!" said the girl on the chair, surveying the charcoal-coated room.

The other woman noticed August at the door. "You, open the door to its fullest!" she commanded, "whoever ya are."

August pushed the door open and rolled one of the rotting turnips over with her foot to hold it there. *Turnip doorstop. Practical. Add to the new list: Try other foods, like turnip to see if they send me home.*

"August, that must be you!" exclaimed the girl hopping down from the chair. She flapped her apron back and forth, her long dark hair waving behind her back. "Shelia, will you start the airing? I'm to take August up to see Angus right away."

The other woman snorted, turned her back to them both, and reached for a broom. August smiled back at the girl she assumed was Bethany. The girl had a stain on the front of her apron, just above her left breast. The splatter looked like tomato sauce. She quickly took August by the hand and led her from the kitchen, down a dark hallway. "Oh, don't mind Shelia. She's always grumpy, and we keep her around because she is such a fine cook. Her brush pie is delicious. I wonder if Margaret has her recipe. You could make it." Bethany stopped to take a breath and continued, "Oh, sorry, August, I'm rambling on. I'm pleased to meet you. Louisa-Ray said you were tall and, gosh, you are like a scarecrow."

"I'm pleased to meet you too, Bethany." said August, wondering if she looked freakishly tall, the Gulliver of the mushroom world. *Okay, focus on your task, August.* "What's Angus like? Any tips for me?"

"Oh, he's all right. He can be grumpy, but he's a man with many responsibilities: a lovely, but crippled, wife at home and twin girls, useless girls actually, of marrying age, so he's constantly trying to make a match within the guild. But really, his most important job is making sure Master Mandlestone has smooth days." Bethany took a quick breath and looked down the hallway and said in a whisper, "His temper explodes like a blazing fire."

With that, they stopped and Bethany held a wooden door open. The room's dampness rushed their bodies. August pulled her shawl up around her neck.

"Just remember your best manners with Angus and you'll be fine. I've got to get back to the sooty mess. Come and say bye when you're done." The girl happily bustled back down the corridor, her long hair swaying like a horse's tail behind her.

A massive wooden desk sat in the centre of the room, with a plush groundskin chair. A broad bookshelf stood against the wall opposite the fireplace. A large rug with woven concentric circles hung by the door she'd entered.

August took a deep breath as the nerves tingled in her stomach, then sat down in a wooden chair beside the bookshelf. *Okay, you're not meeting with an investor to save your company, you're just here to meet a man about some scribe work.* Her stomach settled. *And more importantly, find a clue to traveling home.*

August rose with a start as a petit, balding man with a desperate comb-over came in from an internal door she'd missed beside the hanging rug. The man looked up from the papers in his hand and grimaced, his small waxed moustache cresting like a wave.

"Ah, ya're here already. Ya're awfully tall," he said gruffly, pulling off his cape and hanging it on a hook by the bookshelf. Geometric mushrooms hung in the cape's folds, framed by circles sparkled with silver thread.

August curtsied, just like Louisa-Ray had told her. *I am not that tall, you're just short.* With her head bowed, August said, "My name is August Monk and I've come to inquire about the scribe work for Master Mandlestone." *Man, I am getting the hang of this dialect.*

The man pursed his lips, and walked around August with slow, considered steps.

"I'm Angus McLorry. Where's ya husband?"

"He died, and so did my daughter last winter. Our people came from Marlow." August's pain flared. *Please let Andrew and Ripley be okay.*

"And why'd ya come here, to Faversham?"

"I was saddened by my losses and needed a fresh start."

"I see." He continued his circle. "And where did ya learn ya letters and numbers?"

August shared the story she'd prepared on her walk. "My father was a member of the Northern Fungi Guild and taught me. I was an only child."

"Unusual to teach a girl, but not unheard of... And what have ya practiced?"

"I can add and subtract. I can keep accounts in order and write letters. I helped my father with much of his guild work when his episodes of gout left him bedridden. May the Lord of Purity bless him." *Nice flourish.*

Angus titled his head, his moustache quivering. "I've never had a woman here and I'm not convinced ya can handle the stress of the work… It's a fortnightly position. Ya'll respond to correspondence and tabulate some of the accounts for the sporelock guild."

Do not call him sexist. "I may not have the muscles of a lad, but I have the mental muscles required to do that work, sir."

"Perhaps. Ya certainly have broad hips. How many children have ya live birthed?"

Be cool. "One, sir."

August, nauseous in her stomach, saw a flash of toddler Ripley in her bath bucket on the floor of their shower. She adored the warm water, her coloured soap crayons, playing peekaboo with a washcloth. Ripley cried every evening she was pulled from her soapy water for bed. She'd only settle once she was snug in her onesie, ready for a story.

Angus sighed, "Well, I suppose I could give ya a try. I've been searching for months. And even though ya're a woman, ya seem to have *some* brains."

"Sir Angus, I am grateful for the opportunity." She said, feeling a heat rise in her body, her cheeks redden. *Oh fuck, a hot flash.*

Angus stifled a small smile. "The only sir around here is Sir Hugh. Just call me Angus." He sat down in the large chair behind the desk. "Be here tomorrow, first thing after sunrise. I'll show ya the books and letters then."

"Of course. See you then," said August, desperate to leave, her body flooded with fieriness. After a quick curtsey, she rushed to the hall, pulling off her shawl, opening the tie at her throat, loosening her shirt. She spotted a door beside an outside window, she pushed through the arch to stand in a stone annex. She pressed her back against a cooling wall, fanned her neck with her shirt, the heat swelling in her feet and legs. *If only I could take off these fucking boots.*

Another door into the annex swung open, and four young men rushed out in cream capes, large sporelock crests on each shoulder. Without acknowledging August, the brisk men strode through the annex, their purity boots echoing on the stone floor. One man said, "One hundred pounds to find a Wikka! We'd have enough money to find ourselves a well-placed wife with a dowry that large."

"And I'm sure she'd be aching daily for our hard knives," said another. The young men laughed, in high spirits heading towards the barn.

Oh fuck, they're rewarding boys to find Thread Carers. Does Margaret know? August vowed to make sure Margaret and her friends were prepared.

SEVENTEEN
MARGARET

Two afternoons later Bethany arrived at the cottage, her eyes wide and sparkling, light flushes of pink across her nose and cheeks.

"Ya're here, Bethany. Welcome," Margaret said as they rose from their stool, their mug in their hand.

"Margaret, I'm so pleased to be asked to study with you, but – " The girl stopped.

"Now, Bethany," said Margaret softly. "I want ya to know this is a space for ya to be yaself. If that's questions or complaints, 'tis all welcome here. So please, come and sit down beside me," Margaret said, lowering themselves back to the bench, leaning their back against the cottage wall.

Bethany bit the inside of her mouth, smiled slightly, then sat down. She took a breath and spoke. "I'm just worried that I'm not smart enough to do this. I know you chose me, but I've never been great at anything and I'm worried I'll let you down. And I don't want to do that. So I've come here to tell you, with deep respect, that I can't train to become a midwife. I just don't have the right skills."

Margaret smiled and put their hand on Bethany's shoulder. The worry and anxiousness reminded them of their early training. The constant voice repeating that they weren't right for the job. How could they support women in childbirth when they didn't have a monthly moon themselves?

"Bethany, here's a secret for ya. We all feel this way."

"What, even you? You didn't feel ready for this work?"

"Yes. And this is one of the things ya come to know about yaself. When things are their most difficult, that's where ya find ya greatest strength and sometimes purpose. It's the gift that comes with the seemingly insurmountable."

"Insurmountable?"

"Something that appears to be completely out of reach, like a jug at the top of a high dresser. Ya can't reach it even on ya tippy-toes."

"Ah… Insurmountable. I like that word, but it also… terrifies me. I mean, I'm not terrified like startled but something about it unsettles me, like I've eaten old rabbit."

Margaret laughed out loud and smiled. "That's exactly right, Bethany, the unsettling lets ya know ya be on the right path. I promise that if ya listen well, practice, and be open to the challenges that come, ya'll be just fine."

Bethany smiled back at Margaret. "I really will listen and learn and follow your every instruction… If you believe I can do it, I probably can. Okay… I'm ready to start right now," Bethany said, standing up with a jump.

The vigour of youth, I remember that lightness. "Grand, Bethany. We will get going shortly. And August will join us. I know ya already met her at the house earlier this week."

"Oh, yes," said Bethany. "She seemed lovely. And Da says she's a permanent fixture at Louisa-Ray's and that she should probably get her own cushion for the bench."

"I completely love that idea," said August as she swung open the cottage door, holding two mugs of tea.

Bethany turned white. "Oh, no. I'm so sorry... I'm always running my mouth and Da says – "

"Bethany, don't worry about it. That's not the worst thing I've heard townsfolk say about me," August said, holding out a mug for the girl.

Bethany reached out her own hand. "Thanks, August."

"Lovely," said Margaret, rising from the bench. "I have a few things to organize before we head off for our first forage. And while I'm doing that, Bethany, please get those boots off."

Bethany plopped down on the ground, next to the firepit, and loosened the buckles on her tall groundskin boots.

"Margaret," said August, "do you need help with anything?"

"I'm all right. But thanks. I'll be quick, and then off to the forest."

"That's right Bethany. Use ya fingernails to scoop the little pats of mushroom butter out of the nests," said Margaret.

Margaret was sitting on a mossy fallen oak, Hazel at their side watching the three women bend down in the psilocybin stoop to collect the butter nest fungi. In this part of the deep forest the butter nests covered the ground like a light creamy carpet with pops of bright yellow. The women brushed the collected fruit from their fingertips and wiped them across the top of the small ceramic containers in their hands.

"Oh JESUS!" yelled August.

This exclamation was becoming very familiar to Margaret, and they made a note to ask August who or what Jesus was.

"That gigantic butterfly scared the bejesus out of me! It was like a mottled bird swooped down to attack me!" continued August.

"Were you once attacked by a butterfly?" asked Bethany curiously.

"No, but they're just so freaking big!"

Bethany pursed her lips. "Do you not have butterflies like this where you come from?"

August flinched as Margaret jumped in: "The northern part of the country has much smaller butterflies, more like the size of an ant."

"Mother Nature certainly is full of breadth," said Bethany with a shrug and bent back down to gently harvest the butter nests.

August mouthed "Thank you" to Margaret and also continued to pick.

The women fell into a rhythm of bending, picking, then standing and scraping into their pots. Margaret thought of Sister Beatrice teaching them secretly behind the walls of the walnut orchard, where, barefoot, they would hunt through the web of roots to find butter nests, then the sister would carefully explain how to use their gifts. Sister Beatrice would scribble down recipes for poultices or sketch fungi with her steady hand, as they sat in their hidden classroom under the boughs of a mighty mother walnut tree, obscured from sight. *She'd known my secret, perhaps...* Margaret pushed the thought away. *I must focus on the task at hand. The Mother Network urgently needs me.*

"Bethany, do ya remember what we'll use the butter nests for?"

Bethany pushed some long brown hairs out of her face as she said, "To help ease with bruising and also for soothing sore throats and to help ulcers."

Margaret smiled. "Ya're absolutely right, Bethany."

Bethany's smile burst forth. Margaret could see the girl's confidence growing with every barefoot step she took on the earth and every fungus she touched. *Of course, the Mother Network knew she was the one.*

Hazel flicked her tail back and forth, hitting Margaret's leg in regular pulses. "Okay, sweet Hazel. I know it's time to start," they whispered to the cat, then called out, "Girls, that's enough butter for today. Let us all have a snack and a rest."

ALL THREE WERE SITTING ON THE GROUND IN A circle, dipping their hands into a bag of nuts and taking sips of water from a shared flask. Hazel lay in the shade of a gooseberry bush near Margaret. August's tilted head stared at the trees. *She's no doubt thinking about a way to get home.*

Bethany spilt water down her top and giggled as the liquid pooled on her soft cloth shirt and then sunk in. "These boobs are constantly getting in my way. I spend so much of my days cleaning my own soft cloth shirts, my Da says I should've been a washerwoman."

"Well, ya've got a different purpose than those who keep us clean," said Margaret. "Now, let's try to use the Mother to communicate."

Bethany's jaw dropped. "What, right now? On the first day?"

"Yes, today. I know you're nervous. We're all nervous, especially with the news a reward is on offer, but the best way for us all to overcome those trembles is to give it a try."

Bethany took a deep breath and blew the air out through pursed lips.

"Good, Bethany, that's exactly what we need. Bring up ya confidence. Now, make sure the whole of ya foot is connected to the earth. Ya may want to stand, as it helps when ya first learn."

Bethany rose quickly and firmly stamped each foot into the ground, dust rising up her legs. "Like this?" she asked.

"Yes. August, you too," said Margaret raising their eyebrow at the women.

"Oh, I just thought I was here to tag along," said August as she stood up, carefully placing her soles into the earth.

"As ya're both here, it makes sense to teach you both." Margaret detected a tingle in their feet, as they rose slowly up to their full height.

"The Mother has many strengths. Today we're going to use them as a communication web. For centuries Thread

Carers have used the web to reach each other in faraway places. They aren't complex messages, like ya can send through a letter. They're more like sending a feeling."

August and Bethany waited for Margaret to continue.

"Now it will take ya practice, but my hope today is that ya can sense the Mother. And eventually, ya'll be able to send a message."

"Do we use Hazel to help send the message?" asked Bethany.

Hazel stood up sharply, turned away and, with her tail raised in the air, disappeared into the gooseberry bush.

"Well, I guess not," said Bethany and called out, "Sorry, Hazel, I thought we all got to use you!"

"Ah, Hazel is just for me," said Margaret. "She was a gift to me from the Mother when I became an appointed Thread Carer."

"You mean I might get my own Hazel one day?" asked Bethany.

"Indeed, ya just might," said Margaret with a sense of certainty that Bethany would indeed become a Thread Carer. They could almost see the future ceremony under the Mother oak, the binding of the threads, the crown of fungi.

"Now, close ya eyes to help ya focus," said Margaret as Bethany immediately closed her eyes. It took August a moment longer to shut her lids.

"Think of the earth beneath ya feet. Imagine a deep network of threads connecting every tree, plant, and insect that touches the soil. Now think of ya soles connecting to this web, becoming a node in the tapestry under ya feet. Ya might feel a little jolt. That's what ya want."

Margaret experienced their own connection to the Mother, their body and mind becoming a small node in the ravelled world beneath their feet. "Ya're doing great... keep –" Margaret's voice was cut off by an intense burst of desperation that made them stumble.

Margaret recovered and looked at Bethany, "Ya're a natural, Bethany. I sensed how desperate you are to learn."

Bethany opened her eyes. "You did? I was trying to send joy, but I'm probably doing it wrong," she said with a small chuckle and shut her eyes again.

It wasn't the girl who sent it. Margaret flicked their gaze to August. The tall woman still had her eyes shut, a deep concentration settled on her face. Margaret focused their own mind and touched the connection August had created, felt the woman's desperation to travel farther along the web. *I wonder if the other Thread Carers perceive this.* Another jolt arrived and as it left, August opened her eyes.

The two stared at each other and Margaret knew August was here for a reason, they just didn't know what it was yet.

EIGHTEEN
AUGUST

"Margaret, the water is amazing," said August as she stroked through the glassy green liquid. "Are you sure you don't want to come in?"

Margaret sat on the far side of the pothole along the riverbank. Her silver hair shimmered on the top of a jagged cliff thrust twelve feet up from the river. "Ya enjoy, August. I'm happy with the sun on my face," called back Margaret, hands wrapped around her apron and skirts, pulling her knees to her chest.

August smiled and swam to a large rock, its head out of the water, a family of pebbles at its base, and rested her arms. She lay her cheek on the rough, warm surface, closed her eyes, and a sigh passed her lips. She willed her gnawing sense of abandonment to drift away with the light current.

For forty-seven years she'd carried the weight of the mother who'd abandoned her, the family she didn't know, a whole life lived without her. Her life began at age seven, on the day they found her naked, her feet in the Pacific Ocean's surging waves.

Today, the abandonment was thicker and heavier: a weight doubled with her abandonment of Ripley. *Oh, poppet, I'm coming back. I would never leave you on purpose.* The grief grabbed her, shook her insides, the back of her teeth grit together.

August opened her eyes, the reflection of the pale sky coating the water. Glass panes wedged her mind, a past she desperately wanted to return to, a present she needed to help.

August shoved herself from the rock and sunk into the pool. Liquid cool soaked her naked body, stroked her hair, soothed her heart. She swam hard beneath the water, pushing away from it all. Stroke after stroke, the tension in her lungs grew, the need to breathe leached into her cells, demanding she take air. She pulled harder, propelling herself forward and farther until she reached the edge. With a wet gasp, she broke the surface. Her body took over, breath after breath, calming her nervous system, order restored.

As her lungs relaxed and the endorphins flowed, she lay back and floated on the clear, green water. Soft bubbling filled her ears. A light breeze cooled her breasts, bobbing in and out of the water with her lungs' rhythm. *It's okay. You're okay. We're going to get home.*

She dipped her head a final time beneath the water, and let it cleanse her mind.

August sat naked next to Margaret and wrung out her hair, drops of water falling onto the skirt she'd laid down as a blanket. "Oh, thank God for water," said August. "Even when I'm having the shittiest day, I always feel better after putting my body in it."

"It seems to do ya much good," said Margaret, fingering a tiny cluster of gall mushrooms, their translucent caps and stems reflecting the greens and browns of the river.

"Are those the jewellery fungi?" asked August.

"Ya, that's right. They are."

"And the guild that controls them is called… oh, don't tell me… wait… come on perimenopausal brain, work with me…. the glow guild!" she finished triumphantly.

"Ya got it. These here gall fungi are rare and precious. We're not supposed to have favourites," said Margaret in a whisper, "but I do love these beauties. They can take every one of Mother Network's colours… Amazing."

"They really are amazing they, aren't they, and… fungi are both sexes, right?"

Margaret's lips flattened a little. "Right ya are."

"I guess mushrooms truly are intersex."

Margaret shifted on the rock, adjusting her body as she found a more comfortable spot. "What do ya mean by 'intersex'?" asked Margaret softly.

August threw her head back, her face to the sun, eyes closed. "In my world, some people are born with genitalia that doesn't match the convention that insists we're either male or female."

Margaret stilled as her skin grew pink. August, her eyes still closed, continued, "There's a horrific history in my world where intersex children were forced to live as a gender they didn't agree with. Some kids had intensive and painful surgeries. And all of this done without their consent." August took a pause. "Intersex living and our understanding isn't perfect, but it's better than it was. Seriously," continued August, "if Ripley had been born intersex, Andrew and I would've waited to see what they wanted." As she finished, she opened her eyes towards Margaret.

Margaret's raised shoulders seemed tight, her cheeks flushed. "Margaret... Are you okay?" August asked.

Margaret swallowed, dropped her shoulders and quickly said, "Ah, yes, August. I think I'm hot from the sun." And continued, "We should head back," pushing up from the rock, a grimace on her face as her hip strained.

"Oh, okay," said August, suddenly realizing she was still naked, scrambling for her clothes.

"Ya just take ya time, August," said Margaret over her shoulder. With a sharp wave she stepped along the dirt path between the rocks towards the forest.

"All right..." said August, the soles of her feet tingling.

Putting on her petticoat and then her skirt, August hoped she hadn't upset Margaret. *She can't be judging me, can she?* August shook her long raven hair. *No way. Margaret is the kindest, most empathetic person I've ever met. I owe her so much.*

She pulled her shirt over her head and glanced down at the glimmering fungi. *Add to the new list: Will gall fungi take me home?*

With her bare feet firmly planted on the rock, with a connection to the land, the network, and the water, August vowed to help Margaret however she could; in whatever

AUGUST

way the beautifully wise woman needed her, she would be there.

August thought about Ripley all morning as she reconciled the monthly accounts. Ripley scrunching her little face into her pillow – in a tiny bedroom kingdom of calm and safety.

The inside of August's left arm itched. She put down her pencil and furiously scratched the small red bumps. *Bloody, random itchy spots. Add to the new list: Is perimenopause causing my travel?*

August raised her feet up and down inside her boots, her feet trapped, suffocated. Suddenly Hugh opened the door. August quickly stood up, placing her arms behind her back. Hugh's cream cape swayed as he came through the door, his silver highlights streaking past, some hair tucked behind his ears. Strong and tall, his body was powerful and filled with tension. *Oh great, he's more handsome up close. Instead of hot priest I've got hot guild master.*

Angus also entered, continuing their conversation from the hall. "As soon as Jeremiah brings the carts from Whitstable, we can send the last load," finished Angus with satisfaction. His pleasure changed to annoyance when he noticed August.

"So you're the new woman for our accounts," said Hugh. He looked August up and down, assessing her, his crushed left hand dangling at his side.

"Ya, this is the woman we've hired on trial," said Angus.

"Well," said Hugh, sitting in a large wooden chair by the window, "if Margaret's taken you in, you can't be all bad. Still," he continued, "you are a woman and even with that impediment, I will expect good work. Is that understood?"

Do not call him a misogynistic pig. "Yes, my lord," she said with a curtsey, rolling her eyes as she looked at the floor.

"All right, Angus," said Hugh, turning in the chair to face the window. His eyes gazed to the giant oak tree and the pasture of horses beyond. "Tell me of the Sphere's latest ordinance."

As Angus reached in his cape to pull out a scroll, August turned back to her ledger, willing herself to focus.

Hesitantly Angus began, "The Divine Sphere is requesting a sum of two hundred pounds for the purification of field one fifty-six."

"Did you say two hundred pounds?" asked Hugh incredulously

"Yes, my lord. They say 'tis because the land was deeply impure. So filthy it required twice the amount of purification powder."

"Didn't they say the same thing last month, on the western field?" Impatience rose in Hugh's voice.

"Yes, my lord. They did indeed."

"Each letter we receive demands more of us." Hugh stood up gruffly, and looked out the window. "All these lands, all that we've done. We give to the Sphere everything they ask. And each time they ask, they take even more."

"My lord, I believe they have need of the funds for their Wikka pamphlets. The latest features a naked woman, riding backwards on a virile stallion. It's proving popular with many, especially the young men."

August noticed she'd stopped writing, her pulse fast at the mention of Wikka. Sharp, metal taps from Hugh's boot kept time with her heart.

"I need to meet with Father Gerard," said Hugh suddenly.

"My lord, that will prove difficult. The father…"

"Angus, I don't care how difficult it is. Tell Gerard I want to speak with him. If he wants sporelock for his purity houses, he'll meet with me."

"Very well, my lord," said Angus. "I'll send a dispatch right after we meet with the maister. He has birthing precautions for Yvonne that require your approval."

Hugh turned from the window, his lips clenched. "Very well. Let's see what Maister Herge has planned."

As the men left the room, August willed herself to stare at the ledger. Angus gave her a brief "Get back to work" glare as he shut the door.

August sighed and leant back in her chair, placing her pencil on the table. For a moment she'd forgotten about getting home. Instead, she worried Louisa-Ray was right: that Margaret may be in danger.

NINETEEN
MARGARET

THE ANIMALS APPEARED FIRST IN THE CIRCLE OF fungi. The mushroom ring grew beneath six-foot tall, sturdy fungal trees called River Elders, ancient riverbank protectors.

It was just after dusk and a short, squat duck with swathes of deep red waddled into the clearing. Its bill swayed back and forth and then it sat still, listening deeply. It let out a single quack, and the rustling began.

Hazel arrived and sat down quickly, licking her left hind leg, looking bored. A tiny mouse scurried into the clearing and settled under the shelter of the duck's body. Simultaneously, a badger and a crow appeared across the river. The badger splashed her way through the gentle current, keeping her nose above the water. The crow floated on the night breeze and landed on the bottom limb of a River Elder. The last to arrive was a squirrel who barrelled down an oak tree and flung itself into the fungi circle like a contortionist.

All the animals came to stillness, their paws or claws

touching this land. They each sent a deep, rhythmic vibration through the network, whispered words to their Carers, "It's safe."

Slowly, women emerged into their sacred place, reunited with their animals and sat on the forest floor, surrounded by a circle of hendrix mushrooms. Margaret gazed up at the closest River Elder; it rose like a great stalk of wheat and unfurled into a brown canopy. They placed their hand on the sacred mushroom stalk and smiled as Hazel curled up in their lap. Margaret took a breath and opened the meeting.

"The day before the Herding of the blood moon, we come together to thank,

"The women who carried the knowledge before us,

"To honour our sisters who work together for our community,

"To celebrate the threads that connect us to our past, our present, and our future."

The group replied, "We promise to care, protect, and support the Mother Network."

After a moment of quiet, a woman with sandy hair raised her arm to the sky. The crow resting on a River Elder's branch flew down and softly landed on her shoulder. As the woman lowered her arm, she said, "How is it that every time we sisters meet, my shoulder is more sore?"

The circle laughed and a woman giving her squirrel a nut in her palm said, "Well, I've figured out a new ointment for you to try, Lauren. It should help with that shoulder."

Margaret looked at their trusted circle. The five women they'd known the longest, they trusted the most, and depended on for almost everything.

They thought of the horrible message they'd received through Hazel as they sipped their morning tea:

Margaret, our sister Rebecca was taken by the Sphere. Another burning, so quickly after the last, has occurred. The Sphere's texts spread rapidly.

Tears trickled from Margaret's eyes. *Rebecca, she was so young – only a newly appointed Thread Carer.*

Her life was brief and yet she gave so much to us. We know more burnings are coming. We must speed up the knowledge transfer. It is vital we don't lose everything they've learnt. We must keep the balance.

I understand.

Guide our sister Thread Carers at the circle tonight. They need your wisdom, as do we all.

Hazel's paw moved and cancelled the connection.

Margaret pushed the discomfort and pain away from their throat and said, "Before we discuss new ointments, thank ya, Jane, let's start with the terrible news we received this morning."

The energy of the fungi ring, the women, and the animals shifted; eyes darted; a sense of unease grew. Doesjka, her hand rapidly patting her duck's feathers, spoke quickly. "I can't believe Rebecca is gone. She was *only* fourteen years."

Margaret gathered their strength. "Doesjka, we are all deeply troubled. The Mother themselves knows more burnings are coming."

"I don't think we should meet anymore," blurted out Doesjka, the tension and terror rising in her voice. She looked around frantically. "What if they're watching us right now?"

Not only is the fire coming for us, but it is also inside our very beings. We must stay calm. We must protect the Mother. "Sister Thread Carers," Margaret said, "we're all scared. I see each of you here and I value your courage and strength to meet, even when the Divine Sphere seems so close." The women murmured, and Margaret continued, "But we *are* connected. We *belong* to each other, to our communities, and to the web beneath our feet. *We* are the ones selected to keep the balance between the fungi, the land, and our bodies. We have been given the gift to truly understand the Mother. With this comes a rich responsibility."

Suddenly Doesjka shrieked, "It could be any of us next! It could be me!" The woman clasped her shaking hands over her mouth, sobs poured from her body, filling the air of the fungi circle. Each familiar ran, hopped, waddled, scurried, and flew towards the women's distress. The squirrel, small and warm, nuzzled against Doesjka's back. Each animal, with a powerful gaze, passed on their strength and courage.

It was quiet except for Doesjka's grief. With a hiccup and an enormous sigh, her tears stopped. Wet lashes framed her red eyes. "Thank you, sisters and familiars," she said, touching each animal gently, one by one. "I needed that."

The tallest woman in the group, Olive, spoke. "Margaret is right. We each have a gift of great significance." The woman's curly black hair framed her dark complexion. She continued, her badger sitting attentively by her side, "We are the lucky few who get to *truly understand* the great connections of this world, to peer into other times and places that bind us together. We receive expert knowledge from the Mother and use it for a stronger, braver, and kinder world. A world of balance. A world of sharing, not secrets and shame." She took a pause, then continued, "The Sphere can try to upset the balance, set our communities against one another, spread shame, and destroy the life in our lands. But as long as we remain strong, harness our sturdy tapestry of experience and empathy, we'll overcome any thunderstorm, lightning strike, or burning the Sphere brings to us. Let us rise and commit to the Mother," said Olive, her strong Black arms reaching to the Carers beside her, grasping for Jane, wrapping her fingers around Margaret's.

Each woman, bodies connected to the soil and hands to each other, spoke with purpose and loud brevity, "We promise to care, protect and support the Mother."

And while five women in the circle felt a renewed sense of commitment, Margaret knew their universe had shifted. *My secrets, my lies... I am unworthy of my sisters and their bravery.* Margaret shut their eyes and briefly imagined unburdening themselves, freedom from their shadows, a lightness in their soul.

When they opened their eyes, the weight returned with the monumental tasks before them: the powerful need of the Mother for knowledge, Bethany's continued training, and the support for August on her journey home. They pushed aside their shame and vulnerability. *I must remain connected to the threads that need me. I must be here for them all.*

TWENTY
AUGUST

As the moon rose, it cast a red glow over the cottage roofs. The crimson light crept through curtained windows, wrapped its fingers around tree trunks and fungal stems. Village parents wrestled toddlers, donned crying babies, and calmed down excitable youth, as everyone sealed up their homes and buisnesses with wooden planks. The creaking elders gathered warm clothes for the coming night outside.

August raised her head to the sky to take in the tall wooden structure called the perch. *It's like a fire tower.* With a thud to her back, Louisa-Ray encouraged August to get climbing the steep wooden staircase. She pulled on the straps of her backpack to secure their precious night items and put her hand on the grooved wooden handrail and took her first step. Grace giggled behind as they climbed the stairs, her little body swaying back and forth in Louisa-Ray's carrier.

It took them about five minutes to reach the enormous wooden platform sheltered by a huge triangular roof. A large, screened area housed the bathroom and right next to it was a large brazier nestled on a bed of fungi August didn't recognize. "Ah, that's a wee fire we set up for the elders. They take the cold much harder," said Louisa-Ray, gently swaying back and forth as Grace murmured bedtime noises.

"Oh aye, be careful, Jeremish, with that there ale. It's all we've got," she called towards the man hauling casks of ale to the platform by rope and pulley.

"All accounted for," called a woman down the stairwell to four young men sitting at the bottom. Each grabbed a hammer from their belt to dislodge the stair planks. From the ground, they dismantled the bottom step, and continued up the staircase to the first landing. The villagers were safe on the high perch, and when needed, great shades were pulled down to protect them from animals that might herd by air.

Margaret, who'd arrived earlier, helped a mother set her six children to bed in hushed voices. A thread of tension ran through the tower as each family settled with their backpacks and blankets. Children shushed by parents, babies fed and soothed. Everyone waited.

Margaret finished her rounds with shoulder squeezes and cheek kisses and sat beside August. "Looks like we're ready," she said.

"And you *really* don't know which animal is going to herd?" asked August quietly.

"'Tis true. The Mother Network likes to keep her secrets," Margaret replied, her eyes lowered.

Slowly, a rushing sound rose from the forest, like a thick stream parting the undergrowth. Twigs snapped and plants rustled, pushed aside by small, agile paws. Six villagers scrambled up ladders to the lookouts, mini platforms, for better sight lines. "What is it?" called a timid voice.

The rushing sound became a rumble. "Not sure yet," called one of the young women from the northern lookout, "but 'tis not a creature of flight. No need to roll down the covers. The dust and spores are rising from the ground."

Margaret pushed August's elbow. "Go see. Ya never forget ya first Herding."

August stood, wove through families shaken by the noise, and joined the other curious ones gripping the waist-height barrier and looking to the trees.

Wet, black noses popped out from tree trunks along the edge of the forest, followed by a silken stream of rust. The crimson river flowed across the earthen floor, obscuring leaves, soil, and fungi. "FOXES," came a yell from the lookout as thousands of foxes exploded from the woods, a rolling mass of rusted fur flecked with black and white. They filled the streets and flooded beneath the tower, their coats a lake of rusty blood.

The musky and slightly sweet scent reached August's nose as the Herding continued to rumble. *Whoa, Tabatha would love this! Foxes!* And then a roll of sadness swelled in her belly, her best friend not here to see the powerful wave. She heard Louisa-Ray ask, "Are you okay, luv?"

"Yeah, I'm okay. It's just so... magical, I guess," said August, unknowingly picking at the glistening skin on her cheek, something she did to calm her mind.

With a look into Lousia-Ray's deep green eyes, she yearned to tell her everything about her world: Tabatha, Ripley, the business, the stress and demands, Andrew, her excruciating need to get home. But she didn't want to burden her. This strong, single mother who used her alehouse to support others, didn't need any more weight.

"Okay," said Louisa-Ray slowly, "but if there's anything you want to talk about, I'm always here, with this wee munchkin." She gently pat the warm lump on her back and added, "Well, let's get drinking some of this here ale and enjoy our night."

The atmosphere of the perch shifted as the villagers' anxiousness flooded away with the foxes, their numbers decreasing. With the ale casks opened, August sipped from her cup and caressed Grace's cheek with her other hand.

An elder, named Jacob, whose delicate fingers collected gall fungi, also used his nimble fingertips to strum an ancient song on his guitar. He sang of the first Herding, the great herding of rats. How the town became overwhelmed until a young man sacrificed himself and led the army of rats away.

Margaret put her arm around August's shoulder and whispered, "Magic is just a word for something we can't explain."

August smiled at Margaret. *You're not wrong, Margaret. This entire world is filled with things I can't explain, especially how to get home.*

As the blood moon faded and the light trickled into the sky, the foxes thinned out. A soft hammering echoed as the young men put back the wooden stair planks. And when the sun broke over the horizon, it cast a haze that seemed to dissolve the last few foxes trotting through the village. The Herding was over.

Parents carried their sleeping infants in an arm, or over their shoulders as they climbed down the staircase, hopeful of a few restful hours in their beds. The eldest villagers used the supportive hands and arms of neighbours to reach the ground safely.

Clusters of soft, rust-coloured bodies lay around the village and peppered the forest floor like carpet. Parents reprimanded lively children as they prodded the carcasses with sticks and pushed their kids to a safe distance. August, along with the young children, watched with open jaws as the fox bodies shrunk down. The insides withered away, fell in on themselves, and transformed into tiny blue fungi capped with gold.

The young woman from the lookout put on thick, groundskin gloves and moved from gold cap to gold cap, gently twisting off the circular top, the stem retreating down into the network below. As she placed each sparkling cap in her bucket, the woman whispered something August didn't hear, her thoughts fixed on the fungi. *Add to the new list: Is the golden capped blue mushroom my way home?*

August rushed off to find Margaret. She needed to know everything about these glittering golden and blue mushrooms.

TWENTY-ONE
MARGARET

IN THE EARLY MORNING MARGARET DASHED through the forest, their hip aching. Hazel pushed ahead, like she was clearing the path, easing the way into the darkness, a silent guide for Margaret to follow.

After a long hour of cat paces, Hazel sat down by an enormous oak tree. Margaret stopped and put their hand to their hip, touched the embroidery along the waistband of their apron, a finger rubbing the soft cloth. Their breath slowed and the redness in their cheeks faded to the pink of a gala apple as they gazed at the ancient Mother oak. *Oh, beautiful Mother.*

Hazel hopped onto a thick root that rose from the ground. Along the bulky bark, a range of blue fungi with gold caps sparkled. Their tiny blue cups, the size of raspberries, grew in shadowed nooks and burst from mossy beds, their small rims dusted with gold glitter.

Hazel tapped her tail on the rim of the large root and titled her head at Margaret. "Okay, my friend. I am glad of a seat." As Margaret sat down, Hazel delicately placed her left paw on the rim of a gold cap and let out a high-pitched meow. Margaret laughed, "Oh, my Hazel. That's a beautiful meow."

Hazel's purple eyes blinked intently at Margaret. She raised and lowered her paw again, sounding the same high-pitched meow.

Margaret hesitated, then raised their veined hand and placed their palm on the rim of gold. They let a soft and high-pitched O from their lips. Hazel joined with a single note two steps above. Margaret shifted their pitch, their O matched, the two friends in sync.

The gold cap under Margaret's fingers vibrated, lit up from the inside, like the birth of an opaque, warm bulb. The glittering golden rim spun slowly, gently massaging the tips of Margaret's fingers.

A lightness filled Margaret's body, like sinking into a bed cushioned by a billion soft threads. Their body balanced between lightness and grounding as the mushrooms spun.

Margaret closed their eyes and sifted through their knowledge, eager to share. The silver-green leaves of sage came into their mind. They shared with the Mother Network: juiced sage helped women unable to hold or birth a baby. Sage leaves in hot water to soothed coughs and sore throats. They recalled sage leaves stuffed in a roasted pig for the spring wedding of the Kings and Youngs. They'd ferried much roasted pig from the spit into the village hall for the wedding feast. And in a moment of calm, Margaret had leant up against a fencepost to rest. They'd felt a strange breath on their neck and unknown hands reach into their apron, searching the folds of fabric for their soft flesh.

They'd frozen on the fencepost, hearing children shriek as they chased each other. They'd watched the local boy Desmond reach through their layers of clothing, looking for their skin. As he'd reached the edge of their pubis, they'd screamed and bitten down on his forearm, their jaw cracked. He'd howled and stumbled. Margaret had turtled in on themselves. They'd heard the words, "You bitch!" and the whack of something heavy against their skull.

Their eyes flashed open and their hand dropped from the gold cap. Hazel jumped in alarm from the root, the fungi's brightness faded, the twirling stopped. Their legs shook, their heart thumped in fast pulses as they leant their skull against the trunk, the shame swirling through their body, wishing to be released.

The oak leaves swished in the breeze, and they sensed the Mother Network reach through the bark and touch the softness of their mind: *Margaret, kind Margaret, every part of you, even the parts you keep in secret are loved.*

The delicate voice soothed them, as the intensity of the Herding, the rushing through the woods, and the painful stories settled in their body and mind. They'd never heard the Mother Network speak in a single voice – one voice that sounded like many. *I am so grateful to be here with you all.*

MARGARET SLOWLY STOOD UP, HIP ACHING, AND looked at their bare feet, the markers of age across their toes, the thinning skin and the pulsing blue veins. Hazel gave them a soft, slow blink of purple-eyed love. Margaret smiled and took small exhausted steps along the path back home.

TWENTY-TWO
AUGUST

In front of the town hall, five men of the Divine Sphere stood on the entrance steps in their white cloaks of silver embroidery, glistening with power. Father Gerard, gripped his metal staff topped with a silver orb, reaching for the light in the sky. As the capes softly flapped in the breeze, the aging man stood still, his eyes closed, head raised to the sun.

The last few villagers arrived, clustered around the edges of the group as the communal bell finished its last toll. August noticed who wanted to be seen, attentive young men at the front with expensive capveil collars. *Currying bloody favour*, she thought, looking at William, Sidney, and Popham.

The thick metal staff raised and lowered three times, sharp taps on the wooden stairs settled the murmuring crowd. At the back, August leant against the silversmith's cottage; she rocked her head side to side, untangling the knots from the many pages Angus had dictated that morning, and wondered where Margaret was. August stood up on the stiff toes of her groundskin boots, and searched for the familiar grey hair on top of the warm smile. *She's been difficult to find the last few weeks, always somewhere else.*

Father Gerard shuffled forward on the wide, wooden steps and raised his staff one last time as he called out, "We welcome you to this ceremonial gathering to honour our Lord of Purity with the burning of the gold caps. Let me hear you sing his praises."

The crowd gathered their voices and called back, "Purification is the way of the Divine Sphere."

"Divine Sphere this, Lord of Purity that. Give me a break," murmured August, then glanced around, anxious someone heard her.

The crowd murmured curiously as a cloaked brother came forward carrying a white duck, light brown streaks through the dander on its breast. Placed in Father Gerard's open hand, he clasped the duck's body as he looked at the crowd. "Before we begin the purification, we remind you that *all* impurities *must be reported and destroyed*."

The crowd gasped as Father Gerard turned the duck's webbed feet, revealing a third limp foot. He continued, "Every impurity desecrates our Divine Sphere and affronts the Lord." He twirled his staff, showering the villagers with reflected light and yelled, "WE BEG YOUR FORGIVENESS, LORD OF PURITY. WE SHALL DESTROY THIS IMPURE BEAST. BRING THE GOLD CAP!"

August's anger bit the back of her throat as another of the white caped brothers held a small gold cap in gloved hands. He stepped next to Father Gerard and brought the blue and golden fungi to the duck's beak.

The duck quacked as she smelt the rich mushroom,

then flicked her thick tongue to grasp the cap, followed by a great gulp. Father Gerard dropped the duck on the floor, her three webbed feet skittered uneasily.

A trickle of nausea in her mouth, August wondered how long the poor duck would suffer. The duck pecked with her beak between the floorboards as white spittle formed, then dribbled down her light brown breast. Soon her feathered body vibrated, her eyes rolled and jolted until her pupils disappeared; white spheres glazed with pain. Within a minute, she slumped to the ground, her yellow beak coated with foam, her three webbed feet unmoving. "And so it is done. Purification is the way of the Divine Sphere," called Father Gerard joyfully.

"Purification is the way of the Divine Sphere," repeated the crowd. The three young men in the front row were almost frothing with excitement. August glared, wishing she could burn all the eager men with her eyes. *Like a female Homelander who's not a complete sociopath.* The excitement softened as Father Gerard raised his staff once again. "Now for the gold caps!"

Another brother, much shorter than the others, walked down the steps, his ghostly cape floating behind him, carrying a lit torch. Father Gerard continued, "Today we burn the deadly gold caps left by the Herding." The short brother walked three paces to the lone mast rising from the centre of the square. A tall wooden soldier, nestled in twigs and hay, cast a faint shadow on small piles of gold caps, sparkling in a wooden tapestry.

"The Herding tests our resolve to the Lord. He reminds us twice a year to flush the weak and the impure from our homes." When the walking brother reached the mast, he bent down and lit a section of hay with his torch, took a few steps around the mast, and lit another section. "He shows us his displeasure by revealing toxic gold caps. He demands we burn them to purify our minds and bodies in their smoke." The brother completed his circle, smoke rising rapidly, the flames licking the fungi in hunger.

"And so it is done. Purification is the way of the Divine Sphere," Father Gerard's voice crescendoed as smoke poured over the crowd.

"Purification is the way of the Divine Sphere," came the rise of strong, manly voices. August pulled her loose soft cloth blouse over her nose and mouth.

Father Gerard, supported on the arm of a younger brother, gave a last wave with his staff, then slowly led the procession, in single file, from the square. As the last white cloaked man descended the staircase, he flung the dead duck into the fire.

August's rage flared, and she kicked the ground, her leather boot pressed uncomfortably against her foot. *Those fucking men will kill anything they want in the name of purification.*

She shoved herself away from the wall and strode from the town centre, the acidic scent of burning gold caps softening. She wondered why Margaret hadn't been there and planned to stop by Louisa-Ray's. *Perhaps there's been a spontaneous gathering. I could use a stiff drink.*

TWENTY-THREE
MARGARET

Margaret walked slowly home, weaker, but deeply satisfied. Tonight, after weeks of nightly transfers, they'd sent the final drips of their midwifery knowledge: Their technique to turn babies; their breath pattern for exhausted soon-to-be mothers; the warm poultice they used to ease along the second birth.

They looked down at their tired feet. *Ya've been the most loyal and dependable connectors we could ask for.*

As they planned their cup of settling tea, they noticed a small cask by the cottage front door. It was bound with rope and interweaved among the coils was a label of soft cloth, marked "Margaret Wise, the cottage by the stream, Faversham, Kent."

Margaret recognized the small and delicate handwriting of Sister Beatrice. Their mentor and friend had retired to a small German town, where she trained Thread Carers in the Black Forest. *A letter I expected, but a barrel...*

Margaret forgot the ache in their feet and excitedly peeled the rope away and pulled the top off the small cask.

Inside was a letter wedged between two sacks tied with twine. Margaret pulled out the letter, scented of rich earth and sea salt. *Let me settle before I treat myself to a visit with Beatrice.*

With their fennel tea, marigold balm on their feet, sitting on their favourite bench, they slit the letter with the small knife from their belt.

> Dear Margaret,
> I hope this finds you well, my friend, and enjoying the change from thick heat to the relief of turning leaves.
> First, your surprise from the Black Forest! It's a new gift from the Mother we're calling hops. After much experimentation, we've added it to the ale making process.
> The flavour is more delightful than any ale we've created and, a word of warning, it is strong! Sister Heidi, our most talented brewer, can drink mug after mug of ale with minor effect. After three mugs of this new brew, she was skipping about the kitchen,

kissing everyone on the lips and cheeks. We did laugh!

To warn future patrons, we call the new liquid "bier" after the Latin word bibere, "to drink." Most folks in the village and surrounding region are quite taken with our bier. We've earnt more in the last two months with sales than we did last year!

Not only is the taste and effect powerful, but the bier stores for many months before it sours, which makes sending it away for sale possible, but difficult. It takes many of our carers much time to grow, prepare, brew, and bottle the bier. Plus great care must be taken with the quantities and process: It's part dedication, part magic, and part connection, as all good recipes are.

Now that we've uncovered the power of this plant, I knew I must share it. I've enclosed a bag of the dried hops to brew and flavour the bier. The second bag contains a few root cuttings. I hope they've reached you. Many deliveries and letters are being seized by the Divine Sphere. But I believe the Mother will protect their journey over the salty *sea from my hands in the Black Forest to yours in your dear cottage.*

This monthly letter has been harder than others to write. My hands and wrists have been sore for many years, but now my mind also complains. But I feel a completeness to my life at eighty-four rich years and I'm looking forward to meeting our Mother whenever they are ready.

I wish you and yours much love and courage,

Beatrice

P.S. I've enclosed written instructions from Sister Heidi on the use and propagation.

MARGARET SLOWLY PUT THE LETTER DOWN. They wondered if these were the last words they'd read from Sister Beatrice.

"But I feel a completeness to my life." Margaret savoured this phrase. The sentence rolled on their tongue and settled in their heart. They also noticed this; A similar day of completeness - the last strands of their knowledge safely stored with the Mother Network, ready for future Carers, others wanting to guide and support a balance in the world.

They felt a lift and a grounding. The weight and worry of their task finished, they took a sip of tea and pressed Beatrice's letter to their heart.

TWENTY-FOUR
AUGUST

"Where did you get these *hops*?" asked August, running her fingers through the dried flowers.

"They came from Sister Beatrice. With great effort, she says they become bier, a strong ale. I've got the letter here. Let me get it."

August bit her lip. Her brain tingled. She watched Margaret locate a book and pull a slip of paper from its pages, like a boring magic trick. The tingling became a tickle. Small hairs on her arms raised to attention as a wave of pulses travelled from her feet up to her head. "Oh. My. God," said August softly.

"Here," said Margaret, showing August the paper. "This is the recipe. It's many steps to make bier."

"Margaret," said August coolly, excitement fizzing in her eyes. "Do you know what this means?"

"Bier in our future?"

"Not just that," paused August dramatically. "I'm going home."

Margaret quizzically tilted her head. "How do ya know this?"

"It's obvious," exclaimed August, her voice rising. "All this time I've been drinking ale to get home, but it wasn't *ale* that sent me here. It was *beer*!" August raised a palm of dried hops to her lips and kissed it. "Magical, powerful beer. These wonderful hops are going to send me home!"

August placed the hops to her nose. *They smell like home.* She jiggled her hips and howled with laughter. "It was *beer*! Bloody, beautiful *beer*!"

A contagious smile spread across Margaret's face.

"Margaret, it's blooming *beer*!" August said, grabbing both Margaret's hands, dried cones tumbling down her apron, settling on the floor.

"I am glad of it, August. And if these here hops will send ya home, do ya think we should look after them?" Margaret asked, pointing to the dried florets on the dirt.

August looked down. "Oh, yes... We need every single flower to make supercalifragilisticexpialidocious *beer*!"

With glossy eyes and warmth in her cheeks, August settled on the floor cross-legged. One by one, she picked up the spilt buds, an immense smile crowding her face. "You'll be beer and you'll be beer. You'll be beer and you'll be beer," she repeated over and over, a soothing meditation. *Add to the new list: Make beer and get home!*

August's heart beat with thick, happy pulses. Each beat sending a coded message to the universe. *Poppet, I'm coming home.*

TWENTY-FIVE
AUGUST

The fire in Louisa-Ray's back room smoked, heat gushing from the pit. *Fuck, it's too hot!*

Annoyed with herself, August wiped her forehead with her apron, sweat slicked down her back. She couldn't focus on the beer, her way home. Her mind returned to the letter she'd written that morning, for Hugh.

Angus was away, updating terms of trade with the softcloth guild, so Hugh had called August into his private study. Hugh held his left arm tenderly on his lap, as though it ached, and nodded quickly at August when she entered.

"Take this down, for Father Gerard," said Hugh. He cleared his throat anxiously.

"A few of my youngest men uncovered a massive bed of gold cap fungi in the northernmost woods. They found this growth some weeks ago but now report the breadth of the gold caps has tripled. One young man said there were "as many gold caps as ripples of water in the stream."

Hugh shifted in his seat, a sigh escaping from his lips. "As noted in the terms of the sporelock guild's agreement with the Divine Sphere, consider this letter official notification of the impurity." Hugh paused, then, with coded animosity, continued, "Purity is the way of the Divine Sphere."

Hugh stared out the window as he spoke, like a man looking for a way out. He slowly turned to face August. She saw, for just a moment, a passing of grief, then with a calm and deadened voice he said, "What are you waiting for? We're done. Leave."

Hugh's tone rang over and over in August's head. A voice that sounded like it was giving something up, it swirled with sadness in a way she hadn't expected.

The fire sizzled as boiling water flowed over the edge of the pot. *Fuck, get your head in the game, August.*

Sometime later, a more focussed August had scaled the thirty six gallon recipe down to a manageable four gallons. She called out, with excitement, the beer recipe that would take her home:

"We need forty cups of water,

"Twenty cups of malt,

"Four cups of wheat,

"Four cups of oats,

"A quarter cup of hops,

"One cup of old ale."

August carefully ladled the water into the pot and stoked the fire. As the water bubbled, August followed the instructions from Sister Heidi and added the malt, wheat, and oats. Then she dipped her wooden spoon into the mixture and touched the wet spoon to her lips, testing the heat. *Does that seem hot enough? No idea. It feels pretty bloody hot.* She stirred the mixture and whispered, "Okay, beautiful grains. I think you're hot enough. Do your magic. I believe in you."

"Ya talking to the ale?" came Louisa-Ray's voice from behind her.

August turned with a smile. "I can't help it. I talk to almost everything."

"I've noticed," said Louisa-Ray smiling back, "and I think it's lovely. Now, what do ya need these cider bottles for?" asked Louisa-Ray, placing a clinking box on the table.

"We need it for our beer."

"I like that wee name, 'beer'... Is that because it's got these new hops in it?"

"Yep, hops equals beer. Beautiful, magical, inspiring beer."

Louisa-Ray laughed as August spun in a circle, her ladle dripping liquid on the floor. "Ya sure are excited about this beer. I've never seen ya so happy. It looks lovely on ya."

August could only beam. Everything was right.

"Do ya think ya'll enter the Kentish Cup next month?"

"Perhaps," said August. The edges of her joy softened a little at the thought of leaving Louisa-Ray, Grace, Bethany, and Margaret behind.

"Och, I reckon ya will enter. There's no challenge put in front of ya that ya don't tackle. Ya're a bit of a wonder, August."

August reached for Louisa-Ray's hand. She held it, storing in her memory the rough fingerprints and the faint aroma of rosemary in her red locks. "You're also a bit of a wonder, Louisa-Ray, especially letting me learn to make beer in your kitchen."

"Learn is right. Is ya beer supposed to do that?" asked Louisa-Ray, nodding to the fireplace.

"Fuck!" yelled August, the mixture spilling over the pot again, each sizzle reminding August she was still so far from home.

Days later, August was still trying to make beer. In a large wooden barrel, next to the fire, she smashed the heated grains and water with a giant paddle, her red face glowing. *Perimenopause and brewing do not mix.* She remembered when she and Andrew accidentally gave Ripley heat exhaustion: the blisteringly hot day walking the harbour for the naval parade, the sunshade on the stroller too small. Ripley's smile softened in her mind, the details slipping away, panic rushing her body.

August stamped her feet, flushing the panic out, and focussed on the hot mashed mixture. "Margaret?" called August, smashing the grains with the paddle.

Margaret appeared in the doorway with a box, her grey curls falling around her face. "I'm here," she said, placing the carton on the table.

"Can you help? We need to strain the mash. And after the disastrous one-woman attempt, I need more than two hands to filter this liquid."

Brewing beer was, as Sister Beatrice had written, difficult. August's usual spontaneous gusto resulted in little success. The first batch of "beer" tasted like mud and the second, third, and even fourth were only slightly more drinkable. August couldn't give up. Instead she'd modelled Margaret's thoughtful and organized approach to her work. August measured, recorded, and noted each batch's successes and failures in a book Margaret bound for her. On the cover of the small leaflet Margaret had written, "We believe in ya." August's heart ached each time she opened the pages.

Margaret brought a wooden bowl and a large ladle over to August. "Do you want me to strain out the grains with this?" she asked, holding up the wooden ladle with small holes.

"Yes, please," August said, methodically stirring the water.

Margaret placed the ladle into the mixture at the top of the wooden barrel, accidentally banging the barrel's hot edge. Margaret stumbled forward and, with a flailing hand, reached out to support herself and her sore hip. August watched the fall in slow motion, the ladle catching the edge of the barrel, Margaret stumbling forward, reaching to brace herself, her hand touching the steaming barrel of mash. The wooden barrel tipped towards the fire and fell on its side. Long streamers of boiling liquid soaked the fire, while other waves of hot fluid splashed off the hearth and soaked Margaret. A dripping Margaret howled, the many layered skirt and apron saturated with boiling water. Hot liquid pressed against the skin of her thighs, her legs, and her crotch.

August lunged towards the howling, frightened by the

intensity of the noise from her calm carer. "MARGARET, GET YOUR CLOTHES OFF," yelled August as she grabbed for any piece of the hot, wet cloth she could grasp through the steam.

The howling turned to screams as the boiling water soaked into Margaret's skin. August rushed, her hands shook and slipped against the hot, wet fabric. Grabbing Margaret's waist, she spun the woman, grabbed her skirt ties, and yanked, hard.

The ties gave way as the skirts dropped to the floor, exposing Margaret's pale legs. Her flat bottom shook as red splotches grew around her hips and snaked along her veiny skin. Margaret screamed louder. August stepped backwards, worried she'd somehow hurt Margaret even more.

Margaret grabbed the pile of smoking hot fabric on the floor. Clutching the wet clothes to her body, she ran from the room whimpering, racing to the back courtyard. "Margaret, we need to put a salve on that burn!" called August, confused by Margaret's jolt. *She must be in shock.*

August blinked in the afternoon light, a burning odour hung in the courtyard. Margaret huddled behind a pile of empty ale barrels. Her eyes peeped over the casks. With a voice of shame, Margaret yelled, "Get *away* from me, August!"

"But I need to check your burns."

With a stony voice, almost unrecognizable, Margaret replied, "August, let me be clear. Get away from here."

"Okay," said August shakily as she turned towards the kitchen. After a few steps, she stopped and looked back. The stinging clarity of Margaret's unblinking hazel eyes told August to leave.

AUGUST

August cleaned the soaking ash and ruined beer. Everything seemed wrong. Margaret. The beer. An uneasy tingle in her feet. *Mother, is that you?* August shook her head roughly. "Get back to work; you're running out of hops," she said, pushing down the uneasy crackle of worry in her mind.

TWENTY-SIX
MARGARET

Margaret sobbed behind the ale casks as dark red splotches formed on their thighs, rising in minor bumps like a brand. They hesitantly lifted their wet softcloth and recoiled, their double sexes engorged by the painful heat. In agony, they detected a softness against their bare back, a moment of tenderness. "Oh, Hazel, I'm a mess," they sobbed, seeing the black tail.

Circling their body, the cat sat down beside them, paws next to Margaret's swollen feet. The tightly sewn stitching Margaret used to contain their shame unravelled. How the three other girls, behind the walled orchard, whispered and looked away when Margaret approached with a shiny beetle they longed to share. Their bowl of warm water and a cloth on Friday night for cleansing; their panic at exploring their own body, the problem they saw between their legs. The chicken blood they gathered behind the kitchen for their undergarments, to join the group of young girls who'd become women in the way it mattered most.

Their groin pulsed. Burning drips of liquid marked

their thighs. Hazel sat still as Margaret cried, releasing everything they held so tight.

Hazel abruptly raised her nose, searching the air, the wet tip shifting back and forth, vibrating.

Margaret wiped their face with their skirt, their heaving sobs settling, something else stirring. They watched Hazel stand and circle the yard, then trot quickly back and touch their arm. They took a deep breath and shut their eyes - a connection made to the Mother.

We burn!

The panicked voice lit Margaret with fear.

Margaret, help us!

I'm coming, Mother! replied Margaret as they rushed to stand on achy legs, smelling smoke burning in the air.

The connection broken, Hazel ran to the archway, looking towards the deep forest. With pained steps, Margaret wrapped their sopping wet skirts around their body. They hobbled towards the forest, following as quickly as they could behind a skittering Hazel.

The acidic smell deepened in their nose. Hazel sneezed as the dustlike smoke thickened, waves coiling around trees, licking the tips of fungi on the ground.

Margaret placed their skirt edge over their mouth and nose, a wave of nausea rose in their stomach. They couldn't see Hazel, not even an outline. The ground was hard beneath their feet, the moistness replaced by brittle chips.

Surging ahead, Margaret's pain forgotten, the small cat and the Thread Carer stumbled into an unending wasteland of black. "NO!" screamed Margaret and rushed into the large hollow.

Blackened stumps of ancient trees waved wisps of white

smoke. The carpet of gold caps they'd grown and nourished with their memories, their stories, was gone. Hazel sat at the edge of the hollow, her eyes sunken. Margaret's feet, blackened with ash, plodded into the grey desert. They sunk into a clump of charred branches, their body too heavy for their legs. They pulled their knees to their chest and rocked, crunching charcoal beneath their buttocks, turning it to dust. The ground underneath was silent. Death, destruction, and defeat filled Margaret, anguish crept along every vein.

I failed the Mother.
I failed everyone.
I failed myself.

The giant ring of destruction stretched for miles, a black mark on the ancient web they never forgot.

TWENTY-SEVEN
AUGUST

After the smoke cleared from the village, August looked for Margaret, deep in the forest. She headed straight to the butter nest grove, a space she'd felt connected to the Mother, and to Margaret.

She anxiously scrambled through the woods, the dark night impeding her progress, the fragrance of burnt wood clinging to her nose, everything pulling her down. *I hope she's okay. I hope she's okay,* August repeated in her head, a franticness in her feet driving her forward.

August thought she recognized the large granite rock face. Turning left around the edge, she faced a gigantic oak. Its huge branches drooped their tips towards the earth, leaves brushing the ground, disguising the trunk. *Holy Mother, that's at least twenty stories high!*

Stunned and disoriented, August took a breath. A humming grew beneath her feet. "Go," it seemed to whisper, "Go." With hesitant steps, August pushed back a large bough of clustered leaves and nuts to move under the canopy. There was Margaret, curled in a ball, cowering within the sturdy roots, almost unrecognizably timid and lost. "Margaret, I'm here," said August quietly, not moving closer, just waiting.

Margaret shivered constantly in her burnt, wet clothing, dark with ash. *Was she in the fire?* "Margaret, I'm here," August repeated, waiting for an answer.

The leaves rustled a reply, urging her forward, to Margaret. August pulled the salve she'd grabbed from the cottage, and Margaret's other skirt from her bag. She placed the items an arm's length from the huddled woman and stepped back. Without looking, Margaret snatched the pile, holding it close to her body. "I'll give you some privacy," said August, walking back beneath the boughs hiding Margaret from sight and added timidly, "I'll be just out here if you need me."

And that's where August waited, listening to the boughs sing their song and the ash flutter in the wind, a sadness in the land.

August startled slightly when Margaret peered out from the branches. Her face had more colour and less pain. "Thank ya, August," came a weakened voice.

"Are you okay, Margaret? I've been so worried."

"I'm better now. The salve has eased some of the burn." Margaret came struggling out from the boughs.

"I don't know if you're hungry, but I brought an apple and cheese," August said, hesitantly reaching out with the small sack.

AUGUST

"I am," said Margaret as she gently took the bag, her hand shaking.

Margaret slowly sat on the soil and munched her apple, then bit into the hunk of cheese. August asked, "Did you see the fire?"

After swallowing her mouthful, Margaret replied, "Not the fire its self, but the aftermath... Everything... burnt."

August didn't know what to say. Margaret continued slowly eating her food and stared at the ground.

As they haltingly made their way back home, August carried most of Margaret's weight, the wise woman's stiff arm draped over her neck, across her shoulders. August clasped Margaret's slim hand, the skin fragile like delicate tracing paper.

"I've seen you disappearing most evenings. Where have you been going at night, Margaret?" asked August hesitantly, worried her probe might shut her friend down.

"Ah – I've been helping the Mother." Margaret winced as they stepped over a large log across the path. "Things are not in balance." With a wheeze she added, "She senses a great undoing."

"An undoing? Was that the fire?" August asked, trying to settle the anxiousness in her voice.

"I'm not sure, but she said a great change was coming. She needs my skills, stories, and memories." Margaret paused a moment, her breath fast and raspy. "I've worked most nights to transfer my knowledge to the Mother. It is a privilege... but it has taken much. I am so tired."

Margaret's right foot stumbled. August held her steady and gently kissed her on the cheek. "You've done so much for the Mother. I'm sure they won't mind if you rest tonight."

Margaret's bloodshot eyes pooled with tears. "Perhaps you're right, August. Let's get home to a cup of tea."

"Only if you promise to let me look after you," said August in her best stern voice.

Margaret chuckled. "Okay, I agree."

The two women journeyed home, Hazel trailing at a distance, her ears attuned for out-of-place sounds. *Add to the list: Figure out how to talk to the Mother.* August wondered what the Mother, the keeper of knowledge, might know about returning home. But for tonight, it was August's turn to soothe, support, and surround Margaret with everything her friend needed.

TWENTY-EIGHT
AUGUST

After a successful month of beer brewing, the Kentish Cup arrived and visitors poured into Faversham, eager for the spectacle and the celebration.

August entered the hall. Each Cup entrant sat beside their bucket of ale on a stool. August gingerly walked in with her small keg and embroidered sign, "A Taste of Winter."

She sat down on the remaining stool and looked at the seven other entrants. The tall and very slender man next to August tipped his cap at her and smiled. He was missing one of his front teeth. "Hello, lass," he said gently.

"Hello. I'm August."

"Well, nice to meet ya, August. I'm Tom from Whitstable and I have to say I'm surprised to see a lass here, but really I shouldn't be," he said with a chuckle. "This here is my wife's prized recipe," he said, pointing to his bucket with his boot.

"Good luck, Tom, and to your wife too," said August, determined not to be intimidated by the room of men.

You're going to get home, thought August. But her confidence slowly sunk; she'd made so many beers, so many failures. Nothing had worked like she'd thought. No sip of any beer she'd brewed shot her back to Ripley and Andrew. With every experimental brew, August realized it wasn't just the beer itself; the beer had to be drunk under the right conditions. She needed high emotion and beer. *Today's the day.*

The hall's double doors opened and a roar came from outside, where a party was definitely underway. A young brother of the Divine Sphere - *He looks about twelve -* stepped into the hall of contestants and closed the door, silencing the laughter, clinking cups, and musical voices outside. The boy bowed to the room, walked to the first contestant, and, with a piece of charcoal in his hand, he sketched a single "star" on the bucket, then "two stars" on the next, and so on until he reached August and roughly sketched "eight stars" on her small keg. The brother held a small smile as he studied the embroidered sign.

After assigning stars to each ale, the brother walked to the door, then turned to face the room. With a surprisingly loud voice, he said, "You have each been assigned stars to your ale. These stars will be matched with the three mugs presented to the brothers of the Divine Sphere for judging. Blind judging ensures a just and honest evaluation of each ale. Purification is the way of the Divine Sphere."

The room replied, "Purification is the way of the Divine Sphere."

The brother pulled a leather pouch from his waist and drew a piece of paper from the inside. He unfolded it with quick fingers and read out, "Seven stars."

Tom gave a wide smile to August. "Here, son," he called out, raising his arm.

The brother grabbed three mugs from a shelf and sketched the seven stars on the sides and underneath. Tom ladled out three large scoops of ale, one into each mug. Some slopped over the sides and splashed the brother's white cloak. The brother bowed to Tom, an annoyed smear on his lips, then about-turned. He strode to the hall door and kicked it open with his right boot. Noise, light, and colour washed over the floorboards, then disappeared as the door closed. The crowd's roar settled outside and Tom looked nervously at the door. Everyone wondered what the head judges would make of his ale.

Outside tables filled the town centre. Pansy, the baker, made hundreds of sausage rolls and the Divine Sphere covered the costs. The village slaughtered and roasted two pigs; apple hand pies and bacon strips were eaten by all. Some kids had sewn bunting from old groundskin. The lively flags hung between several buildings and draped across the town pump. Straw lay on the ground to soak the early winter mud.

August clenched and unclenched her jaw. She met a hot flood of fear. *This has to be how I get home.*

Everyone else in the room presented before the brother called the final eight stars. After writing on the three mugs, the young man smirked again as he stood in front of August. She smiled, hoping to hide her nervousness as she hopped off her stool and carefully put the small keg on the seat. She uncorked the cask and filled each mug to its brim with her beer, taking her time not to spill. *Okay, my beauty*, she thought, *show them what real beer tastes like, so we can get out of here.*

From the door, the brother said, "And with this final tasting, we ask you all to wait while the judges debate the merits of each. Once complete, the winner of this year's Kentish Cup will be announced."

August wanted desperately to get into the village square. "We'll be out soon enough," said Tom, as she jiggled her right leg up and down.

Finally, the doors opened. Everyone picked up their entries and walked into the joyful noise and fresh air. August trembled with each step.

At the front of the stage, August looked at the crowd gathered for the food, ale, and day of festivity. Everyone was there: Wilf and Ernie from the cosmos fields looked like proud grandparents, smiles shining up at her. Margaret held baby Grace on her hip, her other arm locked around Louisa-Ray's waist. The three of them cheered for her with high-pitched voices. Love surrounded her, and a sadness followed. *That's unexpected.*

Father Gerard hobbled up the stairs with his globe staff and shuffled the contestants. His richly embroidered cape sparkled as he licked his lips and took a deep breath. The crowd hushed as he spoke. "Each year the Kentish Cup is awarded to the ale that inspires courage to our people in the face of impurity."

As the Father's words wafted over the crowd, August

studied the cup in her hand. The head on her beer glistened and bubbles popped, crafting a song that called her home. Swiftly, August downed the hoppy liquid and smiled.

The crowd cheered and then silenced as Father Gerard raised his hand. "This celebration, made possible by the generosity of the Divine Sphere, reminds us that the Lord of Purity is the one who brings light to the darkness. And today he gifts us the most glorious ale. Purification is the way of the Divine Sphere."

The crowd called in return, "Purification is the way of the Divine Sphere."

I'll be glad to never hear the words 'Divine Sphere' again, thought August, shaking slightly. Her hand holding the cup crinkled with sweat and sourness circled her throat. *Is this the nausea that comes with travel?* she thought hopefully. The crowd cheered again as Father Gerard said, "By the power of the Lord of Purity, I declare this year's Kentish Cup winner to be… ale of eight stars."

The crowd gave a tremendous roar, scanning the ale brewers for the eight shining stars. August heard gasps and more cheering. A shiver ran through her body. *OH MY GOD I'VE WON. I'M GOING HOME.*

"Brewer of eight stars, please step to the front," said Father Gerard over the roar of the crowd. August could hear the distinct bellow of Louisa-Ray and Margaret. Hesitantly, she stepped forward, waiting for a jolt or a spark, for her journey to start. She shut her eyes and willed herself home: to Ripley, to Andrew, to her cats, her sewing machine, and her Kindle. Nothing.

She slowly opened her eyes and disappointedly saw the excited crowd cheering for her; Margaret held Grace up on her shoulders, that pudgy little face smiling at her while Louisa-Ray jumped up and down, her red hair like flames in the air.

Father Gerard stepped in front of August, the golden cup in his hands close to her face. The old man sneered and then raised his creaky voice to the crowd. "Congratulations, brewer, on the Kentish Cup," he announced. And then subtly, under his breath, "I'll find out how you fixed this win, and next year women won't be allowed."

August pushed the misogyny from her mind. She waited to go. There was a loud noise. August tasted dust in her mouth, a dizziness in her mind. She smiled. *I knew it! I'm finally going home.* And then, nothing.

TWENTY-NINE
MARGARET

"Ah, there ya are, luv," said Margaret.

August struggled to open her eyes. It was like something thick and weblike lay over her vision. Louisa-Ray reached her arm to the woman and said, "Let's sit you up, lass."

August sat up with supportive hands resting her against the bench, the fire stoked to warm her body. "Try to slowly open ya eyes," came Margaret's soft voice.

August strained to open her eyes, shut them quickly, and unsealed them again, squinting as she took in Louisa-Ray's back room. "That's right," said Margaret. "Now have a small sip of this here tea."

August gingerly swallowed the warm liquid from the cup and sat back, her face grimacing with the movement.

"Ya took a spill, August," said Margaret, "and whacked ya head something hard on the stage. Ya gave us all quite the scare."

Suddenly a great cascade of tears fell, as August sobbed and quaked in her body. Margaret took one shaking hand

and Louisa-Ray the other. The two women sat in silence, holding August as she unravelled.

Margaret knew how deeply August wanted this beer and this grand ceremony to send her home. And yet, she was still here. Held by the Mother, abandoned by the world she couldn't find. *My heart aches.*

A large clang sounded behind. The women turned as Father Gerard, followed by Hugh, Angus, and Francis the blacksmith came in. A few other brothers in their white capes waited in the hallway. A franticness rose in Margaret's body, every part of them on alert as they stood. Louisa-Ray stood and seized Grace from her crib, the little girl fussing with the sudden start. "Grab her," said Father Gerard loudly, bending on his staff. Margaret's body curled inwards, the need to protect themselves paramount.

Francis walked towards Margaret. "I'm sorry, Margaret," he said under his breath as he held her wrists.

"What the fuck is going on?" said August as she rose unsteadily from the ground, heading to Father Gerard.

Hugh cast his eyes down, his lips trembled. Angus fiddled with the scroll in his hand. "Margaret Wise, you are hereby accused of Wikka craft," said Father Gerard as he nodded to Angus.

Angus unrolled the paper and read: "The charges against you, Margaret Wise, are as follows. One, you were seen on multiple occasions gathering impure fungi in the northern forest. Two, you were seen crafting prohibited ancient potions with restricted fungi." Angus coughed and continued, "Three, you placed this potion in ale number eight, casting a Wikka spell on the judges, leading to an unqualified victory. These three acts committed by

Margaret Wise are in direct violation of the Divine Sphere's proclamations. You will be taken and judged according to the Lord of Purity."

Margaret sensed the Mother calling them, a voice so strong it burst through her metal-soled boots, sending her small waves of comfort. Louisa-Ray jiggled Grace in her arms as August moved swiftly towards Father Gerard, holding her head with one hand. "What the hell are you talking about? You don't have any proof of this! I demand you release Margaret right now," yelled August, leaning threateningly towards the frail man.

Father Gerard laughed confidently. "Oh, I have proof," he said, his smug face glowing. "Now tie her hands," he said to Francis.

August's eyes filled with terror as she frantically spoke, "Where are you taking her?"

Hugh finally broke his silence, "She'll be taken to the cell under the town hall, August. I'll make sure she's looked after."

"Looked after? You call this looking after her! What the actual fuck. Hugh, do something!" August said, almost screeching.

Father Gerard sneered. "There's nothing anyone can do. This is in the hands of the Lord of Purity," he declared and added with a flourish, "and his humble servants."

Francis attached a thin rope to Margaret's wrists and awkwardly tugged her forward. Margaret saw everything slip away as they took steps from the alehouse; losing their pride, their healing practice, and their freedom. Father Gerard chuckled as he hobbled from the room. Francis pulled on Margaret's rope like a farmer encouraging a gelding to take its first steps.

Margaret glanced briefly back to the room. Grace's hand reached towards them, her little fingers twinkling, her face smushed with confusion. Louisa-Ray's cheeks were streaked with tears, sorrow filled her body. August was white with the grief of being here and the pain of this moment. *I love you all*, thought Margaret as she turned to blindly follow the parade of men. As the door banged shut behind them, the only sound they could hear was the burst of Grace's scream.

THIRTY
AUGUST

The village bell rang out in steady low clangs. August and Louisa-Ray perked up, exhausted from a restless night of confusion and grief. With a quick nod to Louisa-Ray August ran from the room, sprinting down the narrow street to the town centre.

The crowd was dense. Everyone heard of Margaret's capture and gathered in the streets, whispering of Wikka. It seemed an impossible tangle of people for August to navigate. *Fuck it. I'm going to push through.* As August took her first steps, the crowd parted, giving her the space she needed to reach the front. Wilf took off his hat as he stepped back with a mournful bow. Hans stepped aside as Pauline pulled her twin boys back. August raced to the front of the crowd, taking deep breaths when she reached the town hall.

The bell continued its steady clangs, mixing with murmurs and morning yawns. August glanced side to side, looking for Margaret, when a teenage boy with a long neck stepped around the building at the top of the lane. A thick hood of capveil covered his face and touched the rim of his white cape. The boy took slow, methodical steps down the lane towards the town hall - a thick rope tied around his waist, the end trailing behind him - around the corner, out of view. The bell stopped as the boy's boots cracked against the early morning ground frost.

At first August didn't understand what appeared around the corner: sagging pale buttocks, hands bound above haunches, a familiar limp. *It's Margaret... she's being pulled backwards.*

Margaret's lustrous grey hair was gone; pin pricks of her roots dotted her skull. A cut over one of her ears bled, clippers having caught her skin. Margaret's bound hands pulled her shoulder blades back, the muscles of her neck straining, her head down. *Oh, Margaret!*

Father Gerard appeared next in the procession. His white cape twinkled in the morning sunlight, while his wrinkled face beamed beneath the crown of gall fungi on his head. Behind Father Gerard Hugh and the five other guild masters followed. Each wore their formal guild attire, crests at attention, their eyes focussed straight ahead. Two purity brothers finished the end of the snaking line.

Margaret shivered in the cold, slow procession. August's heart, already in pieces, broke into smaller, harder shards. August sensed Louisa-Ray join, the pub keeper's soft hand landing on her shoulder, but she kept her eyes fixed on Margaret, willing support to her friend. August focussed on the grey stubble to stay calm.

One of twins escaped Pauline's hard grip and ran to the rear of the train. He halted, his eyes glued to Margaret, and pointed at her with his forefinger, laughter creeping from his lips. A woman nearby grabbed the boy and pulled him to her, covering her loud gasp with a hand. Several others cried out. One young girl shut her eyes, as the man next to her went white and mouthed something silently. *They've hurt Margaret, those fucking bastards*, thought August, her sadness now rage.

More noises rose from the crowd, more fingers pointed. Villagers Margaret had birthed, raised, and cared for turned away as the procession advanced.

Margaret shuffled right past August. Her chest collapsed forward, while her knotted arms thrust her shoulders into the sky. Her head hung low, obscuring her closed eyes. Tears trickled down her face, snot clung to her upper lip. August didn't know what to do; her body tightened, ready to fight or run. Louisa-Ray let out a small cry. August flicked her eyes across Margaret's body, looking for the damage they'd done. Her removed pubic hair highlighted not just a vagina but also a small, visible penis. *What?... A vagina and a penis... Margaret is intersex...*

August called memories together. Margaret never swam or bathed with anyone, always offering to look after the children, or needing a rest. Always covered in many skirts and her beloved green apron. *She... they, protected themselves. Oh, Margaret. Our dear friend...*

Louisa-Ray whispered, her voice cracking, "Did you know?"

"No," said August softly, as another thread of sadness wound around her heart. *They didn't trust me.*

As the trailing men passed, Father Gerard turned directly to August and sneered with satisfaction. Rage grew in August's bones, fighting for a release. "August, no," said

Louisa-Ray, squeezing her hand. "Don't give them the satisfaction."

August took deep breaths, her body uncoiling a little with each rise and fall of her chest. Hugh walked past. His eyes, shadowed in deep black sockets, remained focussed on the path ahead. The other guild masters swept past in their formal wear. The final brothers followed, their white capes clapping in the breeze.

Finally reaching the town hall, Margaret stumbled. Her hips aching as they dragged her backwards, up the steps and towards the main door. Before they melted into the darkness, Margaret lifted their head slightly; lifeless eyes gazed at August. With every connection to the Mother she could gather, August pushed out the words, *I love you*. Margaret dropped their head and disappeared into the black.

THIRTY-ONE
AUGUST

August paced outside the town hall, inadequate and angry. Everyone had left hours ago. Louisa-Ray had stayed with her until Grace had enough, needing her crib and an uninterrupted sleep. The men were still in there, debating Margaret's future. She wanted to scream, or stomp, or just do anything to change what was happening. *I'm so fucking useless!* Hazel sat nearby, alert, her ears rotating back and forth as though she waited for something.

Moments ago Angus had arrived in a fluster to get Hugh. She'd grabbed him as he went up the steps, "August, I know nothing about Margaret. I'm here to fetch Hugh. Yvonne is in labour with the twins." August twisted Angus's jacket arm hard. "Just let go of me, will ya? And I'll see what I can find out," he said, softening.

"Okay, please, *please* find out what you can!" said August, violently pushing his arm away, watching him rush up the steps.

August jammed her feet on the ground, the metal soles of her boots slammed against her feet. *Fuck this*, she thought as she sat down on the steps to undo the buckles, grateful for something to take her mind off Margaret.

With free feet, August stood up and threw her boots at the main door, a great thud as they smacked against the wood. She paced again, this time the cold winter ground stinging her bare feet. She stopped as the door flung open with a squeak and a dishevelled Hugh rushed down the steps, quickly followed by Angus. Hugh didn't notice August, just ran down the lane, towards his future sons.

Angus stopped at August's side, his voice shaking. "It seems Margaret shall be burnt at the stake." And added kindly, "We're sorry, August. Margaret doesn't deserve this. Her calm hand birthed my twin girls. Maggie's screams of pain made me crazy with fear. 'Twas Margaret who brought those girls safely into this world and cared for us after. She's bound many a family together, no matter her sex." With a weak smile, he pulled up the collar of his coat and hurried to catch Hugh.

So that's it, thought August. *Margaret is going to burn and there's nothing I can do.* She sunk down onto the street, the cold and cracked soil pressing against her skirt, numbing her sitting bones. All she perceived was grief, uselessness, and failure. Hazel rubbed back and forth against August's outstretched legs, her tail curling. Back and forth she weaved, a steady rhythm that slowed down August's breath. She reached out to Hazel's dark face. "Oh, Hazel, what are we going to do?"

Tears finally released as Hazel licked her hand. Then the cat sat down and stared straight at August's face. Light snow fell on August's skirts and melted into Hazel's fur.

Hazel grabbed the corner of August's petticoat and

tugged it with her mouth, like a dog taking a toy from its owner. An annoyed August said, "Hazel, I don't want to play."

Undeterred, Hazel tugged so hard with her little cat teeth, something ripped. August looked up as Hazel let go of the fabric and trotted away. The black cat looked back over her lanky shoulder, then trotted towards August and bit into her petticoat again, tugging even harder. *Are we having a Lassie moment?* thought August and smiled despite herself. She reluctantly heaved herself up and said, "Okay, Hazel, I guess you have a plan."

She followed Hazel through the town lanes, the cat looking back every so often to check August was there. August kept stepping, hoping that somehow Hazel would lead her to help.

SOON THEY WERE ON THE SOUTHERN PATH outside the village, the tree roots crisscrossing around her feet. Hazel effortlessly hopped over and around them, an agility stemming from years among these trees. They went deeper into the woods and into a gully that ran along the bottom of the hill. The winter sun's cold light illuminated the treetops, casting long shadows across the forest floor. From the darkness on her left, bright yellow eyes peeped out, followed by a little brown muzzle. A light brown squirrel bounded from the shade and stepped politely in front of August's cold feet. It tilted its head at her, then scampered after Hazel down the trail. August rubbed the back of her sore neck and continued on.

A crow cawed and then August thought, *Is that a duck?* She followed the path around the corner of an ancient oak tree and stopped. Five women sat in a circle surrounded by a ring of mushrooms. *What the...* And then it clicked into place. *It's the sister Thread Carers.*

Each woman sat with puffy eyes or reddened cheeks, a swollen face, or other delicate markings of grief. The women rose from their seats in unison, slowly stepping over the fairy ring and walked towards August, a swirling mix of compassion and sadness cloaked their bodies. Each placed a hand on August and placed their second hand on another sister's shoulder, surrounding August in a protective circle. Instead of sinking into the undergrowth, she was held up by the wheel of the Carer sisters. A buzzing ran through her body and tingled her feet. She heard a hum in her ears, a song that seemed familiar and warm.

For some time the Carers stood in a circle, connected with each other, grieving as the winter sun disappeared into night. When the humming stopped, all the women, except one, removed their arms from August. With a firm grip on August's shoulder, a tall and dark woman with curly black hair spoke. "Dear August, we grieve with you, and on our own for our beloved Margaret." With a squeeze of her hand, the tall woman continued, "Carers, August, please sit in circle."

August watched each woman find a seat beside their familiar. The crow who cawed earlier landed on the shoulder of her woman with sandy hair. A small woman, with one shortened leg, gingerly took a seat as her squirrel nestled into her lap. A mouse hopped into the apron pocket of a large woman sitting cross-legged, then peeped out and blinked at August. A green and gold duck looked for grubs in the dirt until a tall woman said, "Colenso, get over here." The duck quickly scuttled to her feet.

The dark woman stood still and deliberately gazed towards the edge of the clearing, where August noticed a badger resting against a fallen log. Hazel, by August's feet, let out a long, high meow. Every animal joined her. Quacks, squeaks, squeals, flaps, and grunts harmonized with Hazel. *I'm never going to stop grieving*, thought August as the melody brought more tears. As the animals kept singing, Hazel stopped her mournful meow and nudged August to take a seat. Hazel purred as she burrowed into August's apron, settling with a sigh.

The animals ended their song as the badger shuffled its way into the centre of the ring and plopped down, the moss vibrating. "And now that Leith has joined us," said the tall woman with a small smile at her badger, "we must discuss what comfort we can bring to our sister as she ends her time in this world."

The night swallowed up the women and their animals, their grief and their plans. All of them protected by the Mother tree over their heads and the Mother beneath their feet.

THIRTY-TWO
MARGARET

Margaret sat still, cross-legged in their windowless cell, taking long deep breaths, recalling memories.

Dropping off a loaf of bread for young Hugh, the boy left hungry when dear Thomas couldn't rise from his bed. Hugh's eyes would follow their movements around the room, wishing to grab the ties of their green apron and hold tight.

Young Jim, who tried many hot summer evenings to get them in the river. They'd observed a powerful pull to get close, but never been able to reveal everything.

The death of old Joe Collins, the final breath he took that was relief and a new beginning.

The stream near their dear cottage that rolled with bubbles, gurgling in symphony with the bees.

Dried lavender, its crunchy buds in their hands, the soothing scent.

That first cry: new life coming into this world, discovering the arms of its mother and the milk at her breast.

The aroma of the earth, forever pulling them to the Mother, their sister Carers, their loves.

The unexpected arrival of August, a woman with a purpose greater than even they understood, who made a home in their community, even though she desperately longed to leave.

They took the deepest breath they'd taken all day and sighed out of their mouth.

I'm grateful for the time I've had. The love I've received. The love I've given. The joy and contentedness I've been able to find in many a simple moment.

They breathed love in and out as a key tinkled in the lock of their cell. They opened their eyes as August darted into the room, shutting the door quietly.

August faced Margaret, great globs of tears ran down her cheeks. *I'll miss that face*, they thought.

August ran straight to Margaret, dropped to her knees, and buried her face in their arms. "Oh, Margaret, I'm so sorry."

Margaret placed their hand around her back and cradled her head.

"Oh, love, 'tis okay. As much as I hid, I've also known this was coming," said Margaret. "Now ya just take ya time and cry."

August sobbed even harder. Her tears escalated, culminating in a scream-like crescendo, then subsided into ripples.

"That's right," said Margaret rubbing circles on August's back. "I want to explain."

August raised her head from Margaret's shoulder, leaving a wet patch of tear stains. She clasped Margaret's right hand, sitting on the hard stone floor of the cell. August couldn't raise her eyes. "Now we know ya must be fussing, imagining 'twas all your fault, August," said Margaret, raising their hand as August tried to interrupt, "but let me tell you how I know that's untrue." They squeezed August's hand and began. "The Divine Sphere and I have history. I've been running and hiding for much of my life. And here, now, I've realized that cowering is not the answer." Margaret paused as she touched the prickles on her scalp with her fingers. "When I was young I felt ashamed, *so different*. But I also understood I was a woman. I was drawn to the connection and kindness that many females bring to their work. I thought I was to stay in my walled orchard, but when my monthly blooding never arrived, the Purity Sisters worried." August squeezed Margaret's hand in return, as they paused a moment. "The sisters worried, especially when the Sphere wrote a small booklet, called *Wikka of the World*. 'Twas the start of a new age for these men, an obsession with strong, wise, caring women. They looked for differences and the sisters knew they could come to hunt for me, that not even the high walls would protect me." Margaret paused for a moment and bit their lip. "I was sad to leave and I suffered great shame, forced to give up all I knew. I had midwifery and healing skills from Sister Beatrice to lean on, along with a pouch of coins the sisters collected. I carry those women with me always in my green apron, their thirteen names embroidered along my waistband, messages of love to carry with me. With these gifts and my small knife in my belt, I found Faversham and my new family."

August, her face splotchy with tears, said with a smile, "So, that's why you fondle your waistband so much."

"Ah, ya're so observant, August. That's a quality I admire so much in you," said Margaret, holding back a growing lump in her throat. *I'll miss that bright energy.*

Timidly August asked, "What I don't understand is... why you didn't tell me, Margaret?"

Margaret found their courage, beneath their shame. "Well, it's been years of a habit hard to break. And I still carry much shame... " They paused, then carried on, "I'd always worried that if others found out I'm both sexes, they'd dismiss me. I had a powerful urge, spurred on by the Mother, to care, support, and nurture. I worried I'd be cast out, excluded, made an other. I just wanted to be Margaret."

There was a pause in the unravelling and softly August said, "I understand, Margaret, but I still wish you'd told me. I could've helped and maybe we wouldn't be here right now... And if I hadn't been so focussed on my own desire to get home, hadn't won the Kentish Cup with my stupid beer, then you wouldn't have been –"

With a firm but kind tone, Margaret said, "Stop, August. Ya're not responsible for this. The Divine Sphere carried this hate long before ya arrived and when I'm gone it will still hang heavy over their spheres."

"NO!" exclaimed August. "I won't let them burn you. I will absolutely not let this happen. I'm going to demand that Hugh... "

Margaret cut her off. "August, it's not Hugh's fault. That man is just one on a guild council and he already suffers at their vicious tongues."

"What? I don't know how you can be so generous. Hugh didn't stop them from your…" August couldn't get the words out, tears bubbled and fell.

"Oh, luv," said Margaret. "Hugh suffers from a great sadness, just like his father Thomas. Thomas was a man who often took to his bed for weeks. And one winter day Hugh found his father hung by his neck, swinging from a River Elder."

August gasped, "What? His father hanged himself?"

"That's right. The world became too much for our sweet Thomas. Not even his delicate sketch work could soothe his soul from his pain. And Hugh suffers, not only the same sadness as his father, but the shame of his father, his abandonment. The other guild masters mock him for it."

August looked confused and yelled, "Why does it have to be so complicated!" And then fell limp, everything drained from her body.

The teary woman curled up in their arms. The two held each other against the abandonment they'd each experienced, worlds apart.

August snored softly, her head in Margaret's lap. They filled with a sense of relief, soon to be connected back to the earth. Relief they didn't have to pretend or hide. *I have brought much love and kindness to this world, many babes to soft bosoms. That is enough.*

Margaret detected vibrations in their body, a strange

humming penetrated the stone floor. The buzzing soothed their mind and as a whisper in their ear, they heard the voices of their Sister Carers:

We always knew, and we always loved you.

Tears streamed down Margaret's face, shattering the last shards of shame. *Of course they knew... and of course they loved me anyway.*

Angus quietly opened the cell door, carrying a bundle of clothing under his arm. Margaret blinked and August stirred, stretching and opening her eyes. Margaret watched the horror rise on August's face as Angus held out the fabric. "I know 'tis not much," he said meekly, "but I thought ya might want ya apron and some other clothes."

"Many thanks, Angus. I appreciate you," said Margaret calmly, standing to reach for the garments.

August suddenly rose. "I don't want you to go! This is not right!"

"I know, luv," said Margaret, stepping into their clothing, their double sexes disappearing amongst the softcloth. "But ya're okay for me to go now." She winked at August. "I can leave ya because I'm, at least, clothed, not naked like my birthing day."

August also smiled and, after a moment, asked, "How are you so calm about... dying today?"

Margaret took a deep breath. "Well, it's not that I'm calm, luv. In fact, I've excitement to see what comes next.

While many believe death is an ending, I know it is a beginning. I'll become what the Mother needs. Whether my bones feed a fox and her cubs, or a great willow takes nourishment from me, I know I have purpose beyond this body. I just don't know what 'tis... yet." She paused. "'Tis guesses for us all. But I know I've wrapped my hands around life. I've tried to do my best, support my people, and care for the Mother. Today, I know that's enough."

There was silence. No one wanted to move, for this to end. August spoke first and said, "I love you," as she kissed Margaret's cheek.

"I love you too, sweet woman. I know that you, Louisa-Ray, Bethany, and the rest will get through this." With a firm briskness, they continued, "Okay, Angus needs to take ya. And when ya see my friends, give them my love and tell them 'tis okay. We will all be okay."

August moved sluggishly and stammered, "I will."

Margaret wrapped their great bony arms around the lost woman, hugging her deeply, and whispered in her ear, "Ya're just as courageous and powerful as me. I know ya'll get home," then kissed her on her cheek.

Margaret could see August storing this moment, saving this memory for the future strength she'd need. *Look after her, Mother.*

THIRTY-THREE
MOTHER

Mother reached across their web and intuited the insects they needed, that Margaret needed. Small, furry bodies jumped with vibrations, explicit instructions delivered to their soft confidants. We must do all we can.

At the edge of dusk, a dark cloud of intense buzzing rose from the forests, fields, and hedges. An enormous wave rolled from the horizon up into the sky. It flashed like lightning around the village, shafts of black muddled with browns and greys, slashed with strikes of yellow. A giant cloud of purpose-filled bees honed in on Faversham.

Everyone panicked as the bees approached, stuffing their belongings into sacks, rushing to gather up babies and climb the tower for an unexpected Herding. They dropped the thick groundskin shades as they snuggled in for the surprising event.

The thick cloud swiftly enveloped the town. A mass of rolling wings and vibrating bodies masked the sky. The earth darkened as the intense buzzing in the air transformed to a hum. A low bee-murmur grew and cycled like verses, a chorus rose with higher notes. A harmony of sadness filled the land.

No babies moaned and no mothers shushed them. No toddlers cried to be picked up. No old men crankily complained about aching hands. There was a communal silence as the wave of bee song rolled across the land and slipped into every ear. The humming of sorrow wrapped everyone in its pained musical gift and throughout the long night, it eventually lulled the town to sleep.

IN THE MORNING, THE TOWN DESCENDED, AND expected windowsills filled with bee carcasses and furry bodies drowned in pails of standing water. But nothing remained. It was like the bees had never been.

With the bees gone, a sadness replaced the villagers' thoughts. A misery lurked in their minds, popped into their thoughts, as they mucked out a stable, picked up a spoon, or took ale to their lips. A despair for their friend clung to their hearts, along with the inescapable sad tune of the bees.

Word soon travelled that the bees hadn't flown away, but had taken residence in the forests, resting on fungi. A carpet of soft bee hair rolled across logs and ferns and nestled between twigs and stones.

The confused north field pickers could not move the bees from their harvest. It was impossible to squish, shift, or pry the bees from the cosmos fungi on the log fields. An invisible shield protected their translucent wings and fuzzy bodies.

After trying to shift the bees for most of the morning, the pickers gave up and took an early lunch. One of the young men, Snowden, lay on his stomach, careful not to hinder any of the bees and watched them while he munched on a cheese pasty. Millions of tiny proboscises probed the skin of the fungi. The bees worked furiously to fill themselves with a thin fungal nectar, their bodies pulsing with each suck from the mycelium network.

The Mother was humbled and grateful. Thank you, friends. We recognize your immense sacrifice. We will soon welcome you all back home.

THIRTY-FOUR
AUGUST

August's whole body shook as they tied Margaret to the stake in the centre of town. Margaret rested their shorn head contentedly against the old ship's mast the Sphere had commandeered for the pyre.

Louisa-Ray gripped August's elbow, an arm around her waist. Grace perched on Louisa-Ray's right hip, a supportive trio.

Two figures disguised by delicate hoods of capveil moved the tinder at Margaret's feet. With trembling fingers, each man took alternating laps around her body with a rope, fastening her to the pole. A rope snake coiled around Margaret's hips, waist, and bosom. The air left August's lungs as the veiled figures stepped away from the pyre.

Against one edge of the crowded square, the five Carers, strong with ancient connection, held hands, murmuring a soft and sorrowful song. Lauren's crow rested against her sandy hair, its head lowered against its chest.

Father Gerard, his white robe shimmering, shuffled

towards the pyre, the five guild masters trailing behind. Each man sauntered with great confidence, except Hugh. His grey bangs hung over his eyes, hiding them from everyone. The mumbling villagers hushed. The soles of the guild masters' boots tapped against the ground with each step. Father Gerard raised his hands and spoke in a triumphant voice. "Two evenings ago, we arrested Margaret Wise for three violations of the Divine Sphere's proclamations." He took an excited breath. "Upon investigation, we discovered irrefutable evidence of Wikka. Her body is corrupt and impure! Furthermore, she uses this impure body and mind to craft potions and cast spells upon the pure and innocent!" He waited for the shock and cries from the crowd to settle. "Margaret Wise was judged and condemned according to the Lord of Purity. On this evening, we sentence this impure creature to death by fire!"

August didn't think she could watch this. Stand here as her first friend in this world burned. She shut her eyes; her hands twitched as she heard the first flames lick the wood, the crackling on a path to consume Margaret.

"Grut?" said Grace in a questioning voice. August opened her eyes and followed the chubby finger pointing to the fire. Margaret looked to the sky, their jaw relaxed, a slight smile upon their lips. *How will we explain this to you, sweet Grace?*

"I know, lass, I know," said Louisa-Ray, Grace kicking her legs against Louisa-Ray's hips.

Grace cried out louder and louder, "Grut, Grut, GRUT," the words intensifying into a scream as the fire roared with great cracks. *What were we thinking bringing*

Grace to this? Grace's panic rose inside her body, passing through the threads that bound the trio together. Louisa-Ray wrenched herself from August and, without looking back, cradled Grace against her chest and fled into the crowd sobbing.

Without Louisa-Ray's support, August sunk to the ground and she rocked, whispering, "Please be okay. Please be okay. Please be okay."

Hugh's face swam with misery and tears as Father Gerard stepped towards the front of the bonfire, yelling, "Be gone, creature! We banish your impure body and mind from our lands!"

Wailing rose from the villagers at August's sides. August moaned her own pained cries. Soon the roaring flames overtook the crowd's sounds with their power.

August felt a hand on her shoulder, trying to pull her up. When it reached for her again she pushed it away and looked up. Angus offered his arm and said, "Look, August…" his words trailing off as he gazed at the bonfire.

In the air, something fluttered. *That's not ash…* Curious, she used Angus's arm to stand. Everyone in the village, including vitriolic Father Gerard, looked to the sky. A swath of furry insects flew to the square.

As they neared the stake, the bees, their bodies bloated with mycelium sap, flew directly into the flames. Each tiny mouth pressed their teeth against Margaret's skin, a bed for their jaws. Nestled cheek to cheek, the bees covered Margaret, and delivered pain relieving sap deep into her veins.

August thought she glimpsed a smile on Margaret's face

as the bees dove towards them, searching for their skin. Soon Margaret and the bees disappeared, devoured by flame. Bees circling the edges of the bonfire, with no place to land, burst into sparks. A sharp, anaesthetic fragrance filled August's nose. August knew her worlds would never be the same.

THIRTY-FIVE
AUGUST

A listlessness fell on August; she didn't know where to put her hands, or what to do with her body. She tried to read but her focus drifted, and she abandoned every book she handled.

Angus had sent word that Yvonne had died in childbirth and while the two baby boys had initially lived, they also passed some hours later. Hugh was catatonic; he lay in his bed, unmoving, not even rising to make water, his staff turning and changing him every day.

With no demands on her time, no reason to brew beer, she lay in Margaret's bed and gazed at the red robins picking at the winter berries along the edge of the meadow. August dozed for days in a haze of apathy.

This afternoon her thirst drew her from Margaret's bed to the stream. She grabbed the wooden bucket, unsteady on her feet, realizing she needed food. *When was the last time I ate?* She shrugged, unable to consider the effort needed to make a snack. As she walked out the door holding stiffness in her lower back, August saw the sun was already descending, touching the tops of the trees.

At the stream's edge, August heard a grunt from a nearby bush. *Oh shit, of course a wild animal is coming to eat me.* Quickly the bees, the burning, and the burial returned; her throat tightened with grief as she stood up, her bucket full, the water sloshing like memories trying to escape. The noise called again, "Gssshhhh"

It doesn't sound like an animal. Maybe it's sick? She scanned the low brambles around the edge of the stream: *Nothing.* As she turned to head back to the cottage, something flew past her head. Turning back, she saw a hand and its long arm reaching along the ground, peeking from a redcurrant bush. The noise sounded again: "Gssshhhh."

Curious, she mused and, wondering which villager had ended up drunk in the woods, reflected, *Wouldn't be the first time.* She walked towards the wet, pale arm. As she rounded the bush, a sopping wet Hugh appeared, lying on the ground, tangled in redcurrant leaves and branches. "Gssshhhh," he said louder, his salt-and-pepper hair hanging over his face, spit dribbling from his lips.

His eyes were bloodshot and something sticky clung to his lower lip. "Hugh, what are you doing here?" said August, putting down her bucket of water.

"Gssshhhh... " Hugh said, raising up on his good arm and falling back into the bush. His head disappeared beneath the branches.

AUGUST

Every thread of anger swelled in August. She wanted to pick up a stick and hit him. She wanted to scream "FUCK YOU" to the man who'd taken her friend. She wanted to stomp, rage, and throw herself at his sad body, give him her pain. Just then August's bare toes tingled, Margaret's voice rising in her mind: "Be kind," she urged.

"Gssshhhh... " again, now more faint. August blew air through her lips and groaned. Then, channelling Margaret, she reached down to the sad man and said, "Okay, Hugh. Let's get you to the fire."

AFTER A DIFFICULT JOURNEY BACK TO THE cottage, with stumbles and whacks, they sat by the firepit, across from each other. August scooped a large handful of water from her bucket and, after satisfying her thirst, picked up her poking stick. She pushed the stick's end repeatedly into the fire, prodding the logs, moving ash around. Her fingers touched the light blue ribbon Margaret had tied around the top of her stick. "So everyone knows that this is *ya* poking stick. Always poking at that fire like ya're looking for something." August smiled for a moment, returning to her grimace as the soggy, wet outline of Hugh slumped by the fire.

August watched him, the confidence and privilege, his righteousness sucked away. His eyes downcast. August saw a different man, a man lost in this world, untethered from it all and unsure what steps to take.

Oh, fuck me, thought August. *He's like me, just like*

Margaret found me... And for a moment she zoomed back to her naked body meeting Margaret; a day she was lost and desperate, where all she wanted was to get home. August shook her head and gazed back into the fire, willing herself not to stare, but she caught herself glancing at his stretched face, his sallow, veiny arms. The man stared into the fire like nothing and no one in this world mattered. *Fuck*, she thought again and poked her stick into the fire. "Do you have any of your beer? That's what you call it?" Hugh asked quietly.

What would Margaret do? thought August. *She wouldn't turn him away*. "It's in the cottage," she said brusquely. "You can get it if you want."

Hugh stood up, wavering, his pants slightly dry in the front – the closest part to the fire – and headed to the cottage. August continued to poke the fire, listening to the occasional crash and muttering from inside. The door creaked and Hugh stumbled back out with the beer cask in his good hand and a book tucked under his arm. He planted himself by the fire with a tremendous thump. He lifted the cask, pulled out the stopper, and drank from the cascading stream, then set it down. Hugh raised the cask from time to time, taking giant swigs. Hugh drank, August poked the fire, a crow cawed three times. *Keeping an eye on us, Lauren.* A tiny smile appeared on her face.

"What's so funny?" said Hugh.

"Nothing," said August.

A WHILE LATER A MUCH DRIER HUGH HICCUPPED, and then in a sloppy voice, "That is bloody good beer, August."

August sat stunned. *Was that a compliment from Hugh?* She just nodded her head at him. Hugh eventually opened the book he'd brought from the cottage. *If he ruins Margaret's book with beer I'll have an excuse to murder him.* Balancing the book on his lap, Hugh tenderly turned the crinkling pages. He stopped on one particular sheet, and softly ran his fingers across the paper, tracing an outline. *What on earth is he looking at?* Hugh sniffed, wiped his nose with the back of his good hand, and looked up at the fire. His stump cradled the open pages. "It's my father's work," he said quietly.

"What?" asked August.

"This here, it's my father's sketches. Of course, Margaret kept them all this time."

August nodded, remembering Margaret's words about Thomas. His sadness, his hanging, how this man by her fire, then a boy, found his father strung up by the river.

"He was always drawing. When I was young, we'd spend whole days in the forest, studying fungi. He'd sketch and I'd weave, that's before I crushed my hand," he said softly.

"You weaved," August burst out sarcastically.

Hugh's face shut down as he closed the book abruptly.

"I... I didn't mean it like that. I'm sorry." Silence lay between them and the woods.

August spoke again, "Margaret treasured your father's sketches. They referenced them often in training. I know they'd be happy to see you enjoying them."

Hugh grunted, not meeting August's eyes. She continued, "Honestly, I wish I had something to remind me of my old life."

Hugh didn't open the book again, but his body settled. He continued to drink and then stopped, titled his head, and asked, "I don't suppose you'd like a taste of your own brew?"

August sensed Margaret's hand on her thigh giving her two gentle pats, like a child needing encouragement. "All right," said August with a sigh. She grabbed her cup from beside her seat and tossed it over to Hugh. She saw the quick flash of a smile.

They sat for the rest of the night drinking and as the dawn appeared, these two lonely people talked to one another and, more importantly, listened.

Hugh spoke more about Thomas, their afternoons in the woods nearby, and also the days his father went inward.

August spoke about the husband and child she lost when she came to Faversham.

Hugh whispered softly about his failure to have sons, or children, of any sex.

August recounted Margaret taking her in, helping her weave a new life.

Hugh shared the kindness Margaret showed him as a young boy after his father's death, and again when she'd bound his hand after his accident.

They both drank and shared their stories and their struggles while the waning moon shone on this brand new companionship.

AUGUST

THE SUN TURNED THE TOPS OF THE WOODS LIGHT grey. "Well, if you don't open your own brewery, you aren't half the mad woman I thought you were... " said Hugh.

August noticed an ache in her stomach, she didn't belong. *Why would I build a brewery in a place that's not mine?*

"... And it isn't until it's all taken away that you realize you didn't take care for what mattered most," said Hugh grieving.

August came out of her dreamlike trance. She saw a man who had everything – the biggest lands in the county and the highest guild status. And a man who had absolutely nothing: no wife, no child, no happiness.

Hugh loomed, a mirror reflecting a version of herself. Here was a woman who had everything: a child she adored, a daily life of warmth and love and kindness. A best friend who never judged her outrageous sense of humour. Simple morning joys of cuddles on the couch, coffee, and Wordle with her husband. Happiness in the everyday.

"August, it's like you've seen a ghost," said Hugh, August's hand lightly shaking her cup.

I fucking have, thought August. *I've seen the ghost of my frozen past. And my frozen present.* She sat up taller, her spine reaching for the sky. *I guess it's time to live, no matter what world I'm in.*

THIRTY-SIX
AUGUST

When she invited Bethany to live at the cottage, August saw happiness glimmer on the girl's face for the first time since Margaret's death. "After all, you belong here. You belong where Margaret lived," she said kindly, taking Bethany's arm, pulling her through the front door, tossing the girl's groundskin bag on Margaret's bed.

Bethany cried, silent tears ran down her cheeks, joining the stain of blackberry juice on her collar. She grabbed August's hand. "Many thanks." Then, in a flurry, she continued, "I can't wait to get into our healing garden. The new season's herbs need to be tended, plus I need lots of study with Margaret's notebooks, and I need to get a bunch of sage together for Leslie: she's working hard to be with bairn... Ha! That's hardly work!"

Today seemed like the first, truest day of summer. A lightness in the air. August packed a notebook in her bag and smiled at Bethany, who balanced on one foot in front of the herbal cabinet. Her other bare foot rested above her knee, forming a triangle, her hands bashing her pestle with her mortar. *Tree pose is as old as time.* "Bethany, let's get going to Louisa-Ray's. You'll have to finish that later," she said.

"Ack," screeched Bethany as a mustard yellow powder dusted her face and chest.

Bethany coughed and shook her clothing, her hair ribboned with strips of caramel. "I realize I'm not good with rushing and now I've got the yellow fever to prove it!" Both women chuckled. *You were right, Margaret. We are okay.*

"Thank you, everyone, for coming," said August from her seat at the alehouse table.

Grace grabbed August's toe under the table. "And yes, that means you too, Grace. Thank you for being here, sweetheart," she said, peeking under the table, receiving a giggle in response.

Louisa-Ray picked up the girl who'd just discovered the joy of dragging herself along the ground in short bursts and handed her to Bethany. Bethany took Grace to her knee and rocked the child gently. Hugh and Angus sat on August's other side around the table. Hugh tapped his leg anxiously while Angus's eyes searched, looking for anyone in the alehouse who may want to listen in.

"I've been thinking a lot, lately," announced August. "Of course, a lot about Margaret, and what happened..." A heaviness grew. "But also about the future, what we want to do, how we want to remember our friend. They meant so much, *to all of us*. And I've been wondering how we might change things."

"Change, ya say," said Louisa-Ray.

Angus grunted while Hugh hesitantly asked, "What kind of change?"

August reached down beside her and pulled a large sack onto the tabletop. It thumped, clinging dirt falling on the wooden planks. "This kind of change."

Grace, from Bethany's lap, thumped her hands on the table in reply, making everyone, including Angus smile. Grace thumped several more times, hoping to create more impact. "So, what is it, August?" asked Bethany, giving Grace her ponytail to play with.

"It's hop roots," she said opening the sack. "There's five root balls in this bag, which we can plant. And with time and care, they'll give us hops."

"So, the big change you propose is making our own beer, like yours?" said Angus, his voice annoyed.

"Kind of, Angus. But really it's how this beer travels that will change things," replied August.

"What do ya mean, lass?" asked Louisa-Ray, leaning onto the table.

"Hops makes beer last a lot longer. You know how after a day or two you throw away extra ale because it's soured?"

Louisa-Ray nodded her head. "Well, beer with hops can last months, sometimes even years."

Louisa-Ray's mouth dropped. "Years?"

"Seriously, years. Once it's casked it'll keep on shelves for ages. This beer will travel."

Grace rapped her knuckles on the table, aching for attention. The group murmured until Hugh spoke. "You're saying we can grow our own hops, make our own beer, and then sell it, perhaps even in other counties?"

"Yep, and you know where that takes us, Hugh," replied August.

Hugh slowly said, "We won't be beholden to the Divine Sphere."

Everyone grew silent. Even Grace paused her busy hands, sensing a shift in the room's energy. A quiet hung about the alehouse, even the busy sparrows squawking near the open front door hushed.

Are you kidding me? Where's the joyous dancing and cheers – we've hatched a plan!

August broke the quiet. "Well, honestly, that wasn't the reaction I was expecting."

"I suppose not, August," said Bethany. "But the guilds, ale, even the Divine Sphere, 'tis all some of us have known."

Angus spoke up, "There's only a few years of my boyhood I cannae remember without the Sphere and their purification."

August sank back in her chair. "Ah now, take heart, lass," said Louisa-Ray, reaching for August's hand. "Just give us all a minute to take this grand change in."

August smiled at her friend, pushed back her chair, and excused herself. In the back room she poured the remaining winning beer into mugs. "Just give them a freaking minute, August. So impatient!" she whispered to herself. She could almost detect Margaret asking her to still and listen.

Voices rose as she walked back towards the front hall. "Just think of all the single mammies and their wee bairns! They won't be selling extra ale anymore. They could sell beer and make real money!" came Louisa-Ray's excited voice.

"The Divine Sphere won't like it," came Angus's voice of reason.

"They won't, Angus, and they might try to stop us, but they really can't," replied Hugh, his confidence growing.

"I wonder how long the hops will take to grow?" pondered Bethany.

"There she is," said Louisa-Ray, as August entered, beer slopping over the mug rims. "We need more details, lass."

"Yah," said Angus, "where should we plant the roots?"

"What's the process from hops to beer?" asked Hugh.

Add to the new list: Write out the changed process for Hugh.

August shook her head gently. *Add to the new list: Scrap the list – and live right now!*

"Baa. Baa. Baa," said Grace, joining in.

The table fizzed with beer and purpose as they outlined their plan. August recognised a change was possible. They were weaving a new tapestry, one she hoped would break the stranglehold over *her* village and her never-ending lists.

THIRTY-SEVEN
AUGUST

Three Years Later

August walked amongst the hop fields beside Angus's home, Chaucer Farmhouse. The tall bines circled up the poles, small green cone flowers hungry for sunshine. Their brewery co-op had transformed four acres of sterile cosmos fields into rich land for hops.

A large purple grasshopper twitched as August walked around the end of a row. Here Angus bent down, examining the base of a bine. "Hello, Angus," she called.

Angus looked up, his protective straw hat shading his squinting eyes. "Hello," he said with a soft smile, and then settled back to his work.

"Did you find something interesting?" asked August as she walked towards him.

"I'm not sure 'tis interesting, but this bine looks a wee bit damp," he said, pointing at the root.

August sunk into a squat and touched the root with her

fingers. The root appeared soft on the inside and the soil around its base seemed moister. "Yeah, it looks a bit wet here. Perhaps this soil doesn't drain well?"

"Yeah, I wondered that myself. We do have a fair bit of clay in these lands, which was fine for the cosmos."

"Well, the hops don't seem too fussed right now and I don't see any other signs of damp," August said, fingering the leaves as she stood up.

"We'll just keep a firm eye on this here patch," he said.

"Aye," said August, in Angus's rough speech, and gave him a broad smile. "You really have become a dab hand at propagation."

"'Tis something about the earth. It's like... "

"It's like what?" asked August encouragingly.

"Ya'll think me silly."

"Angus, you've seen me say many ridiculous things – I won't judge."

August took the wide brimmed straw hat from her head and wiped her forehead sweat with a green handkerchief. Angus hesitated and said, "'Tis like I can understand the earth, speaking to me."

"Honestly – I think that's amazing. It's a gift, Angus. And Margaret would be so proud."

Angus gave a brief grunt, a rough smile, and quickly set his attention back on the bines, gently touching the budding hops. Speaking to the soil, avoiding August's gaze, Angus said, "'Tis strange and wonderful," then quickly said, "Maggie wondered if you'd come for tea tomorrow, after the co-op meeting."

"Tell Maggie that sounds lovely. I'm off to see Hugh in

the oast house," replied August, putting on her broad straw hat, more sweat pooling down her back. *Will the hot flashes never end!*

August admired the red cosmos building the village had spent the winter constructing. The central kiln rose from a circular tower. The conical roof sat like a party hat, a tilted white cowl protruding from the top. A broad set of tanned hands wrestled with the vane. "Hugh?" she called out.

A large creak came from the roof. "Up here, August," replied Hugh, his voice reverberating through the metal cowl. "I'm just adjusting the vane."

August smirked. Hugh was a natural engineer. Last year, after their second and most successful bounty, the co-op agreed to increase production; they needed more space to dry the hops, more space to make their beer.

August stepped into the oast house and climbed to the second floor. She stood in the cooling room, where the hops would come after the heat of the kiln. The wooden-floored room was dark, no light to disrupt the hops as they settled and finished drying. It smelt of fresh oak and a light breeze through the louvered vents brought the green scents of early summer. August took a deep breath, pressed her hand against the cosmos walls, and settled for a moment.

A door on the other side of the room opened as Hugh came in, wiping his one greased hand on a cloth. He pushed his greying hair out of his eyes with his elbow, wiping his forehead sweat against his shirtsleeve. Hugh's face was light; he'd developed a softness to his movements. *I'm still surprised by his change.* "So I think I've cracked it," he said with a smile. "The cowl wasn't rotating efficiently with the changing winds, so I adjusted the vane. I think that should do it, but we'll see." He squinted in the darkness. "Let's get into the light. I can't see a damn thing in here."

"Agreed," said August.

Hugh rubbed a cox pippin apple against his pant leg and took a satisfying bite. August sat next to Hugh, a lunch basket between them, the protective leaves of an oak tree shading their rest. "Hungry?" asked August as the apple sharply snapped again.

"My appetite knows no bounds these days," he said. "I have not moved my body this much since I was a boy, and my sleep is like a babe's. I had no idea work could be like a medicine." With a smile, he reached into the basket for another apple and raised it to August. "Care for one?"

"Thanks," said August. A sweet, tangy flavour burst on her tongue, juice running from the corner of her mouth. "Oh, man, these truly are my favourite apples."

"A cox pippin is the perfect match of sweet and sour," replied Hugh. He shifted in his seat. "But I don't reckon you came here to talk apples with me," he said, tossing his apple core into the tall grass.

"You guess right. I'm here to pick your brain."

Hugh's smile dropped. "Pick my brain?"

August smiled, "Oh, right. It means, 'Can I get your thoughts on something?'"

"Ah," said Hugh, pulling a pasty from his lunch basket. "Your strange words can still confound me."

August drew a booklet of papers from her bag and spread a section across her skirt. "So, we've forecast two tons of wood for the kiln this year to dry our hops. That's because we used almost one ton last year, split amongst our three dryers and their various houses. Does that sound right to you?"

Hugh munched his pasty. "Sounds like a good estimate. With the tests I've done, and the intense hot heat for drying, it'll be a start. Plus, if we need more wood we've got a wide world of timber around us." Hugh swept his arm across the horizon.

"But – " said August.

"I realize 'Forest management is important.' Honestly, the way you go on about 'sustainability this' and 'sustainability that' you'd think there'd be a future where we run out!"

August pursed her lips. "We do this so we don't run out," she said in reply. *If only you knew.*

"Okay, now that we've 'taken our environmental impact into account,' like you always say, let's discuss something better. Have you had all the votes in for the birthday beer?"

August chuckled. "We have, and you'll *never* guess what it is."

"Hmm... Is it Family Hive? The same name we've chosen for the last two?"

"We have a winner, folks!" said August in her best carnival accent. Hugh raised his eyebrows and shook his head, smiling. "Family Hive it is, for the third year in a row, and I can't say I'm surprised," added August.

"Why's that?" asked Hugh.

"Us. The town. Our conviction. Even when the Divine Sphere tries to set us back with some regulation they 'just found' in the archives, we keep going. We are a family. A resisting, warm, found family."

"I'll drink to that," said Hugh, raising an imaginary glass in the air with his hand.

"Me too," said August, raising her own invisible beer.

"Cheers," came both voices as their air-woven glasses clinked in the oak's shade.

In the silence, a bee buzzed its thick, high moan behind them, hunting for pollen in the blooming poppies. August took a deep breath and sighed. A moment later, a light hand touched her shoulder and Hugh said, "She, I mean *they*, would love this so much. I like to think that, with every bee I hear, Margaret's still looking after us."

August smiled, the tightness in her throat releasing. "Me too, Hugh. Me too."

"AUGUST!" EXCLAIMED GRACE, RAISING HER ARMS, as August came through the archway of the brewery yard. "Grace!" called out August, just as excitedly, picking up the near-four-year-old and popping her on her right hip with a kiss to her cheek. "Where's your mum?" she asked, Grace's red curls bobbing around her face.

"I'm back here!" Louisa-Ray grunted. "Just trying to tighten this bloody stay. Ack! Got it!" she yelled successfully.

"Yay!" cheered Grace and August.

Louisa-Ray came around the corner of the giant beer vat in dark tartan pants, her red hair hanging over her shoulder in a long braid. "Well, that was a grand bastard of a job. It's time to have a beer – for testing, of course," said Louisa-Ray, stroking Grace's hair and giving August a wink.

"Okay, here ya go. I think we've perfected this year's Family Hive," said Louisa-Ray as she pushed aside her notepad with her elbow and put down two pints. She sat down and swung her legs under the table. August raised the mug to her lips and sipped. There was a sweetness on her tongue and then a bite of hops in the back of her throat. "Louisa-Ray, this is magical!"

Louisa-Ray beamed a huge smile. "Thanks, August. Coming from ya that means a lot."

"I'd say that absolutely, without a doubt, you are the best brewer I know."

"Ha!" screeched Louisa-Ray. "I'm the only brewer you know, August," she said with a wink. "But to be true, I've found a rhythm in this space." She gazed around the newly constructed brewery yard stewarded by two wooden vats, new sister tanks named Tansy and Hyssop, expanding the alehouse family. "I spend the days in here, taking notes, experimenting, creating new recipes – sometimes it seems like I'm dreaming."

August smiled at her friend. A woman filled with a purpose beyond wiping sticky ale tables, now made her very own beer. "And I've had a wee idea," Louisa-Ray continued. "Okay, it's not a wee idea at all, but I wonder if we can't somehow share everything we're doing with other villages? 'Tis probably silly but the way it's helped our village, especially the single mothers and fathers, those struck so heavily by life – they're thriving now. And I cannae help but think we could do more with this, help even more people."

"I *love* it," exclaimed August.

"Ya do?"

"Of course I do, silly woman," said August, patting her hand. "I can't think of anything more important than sharing our processes, successes, and learnings with others."

"Well, I reckoned ya'd like the idea, but ya already have so much a going on," replied Louisa-Ray, her eyes cast down. "Ya're building this web that grows each season and raises us all."

"*We* are building this web and *we* are raising ourselves," said August. "And helping others is why we started this all."

The two women grabbed hands. "Aye, for all of us and for Margaret," said Louisa-Ray softly.

A smiling Grace came tearing into the room, followed by Hazel, nipping at the edge of her dress. The two weaved around the table, and headed for the vats. Grace cooed with laughter. Hazel meowed with joy. The two women grinned as Grace stopped, held her ground by the edge of a barrel, and took up the chase. Hazel's purple eyes sparked with delight.

That night, deep in the woods, August watched Lauren, her purple-eyed crow on her shoulder, begin the threading ceremony. Tonight Bethany was to join the Carers, and August was flattered that Bethany chose her to witness the rite.

Gracefully, Olive passed out small green cups of tea. Each woman took her vessel and held it next to her heart. The grassy cups glowed against their deep black ceremonial dresses. Fine lines of embroidered silver thread wove across their chests, like delicately sewn ribs.

Lauren asked Bethany to stand. The young girl tripped on her long black dress as she stood, nervous legs shaking. Jane chuckled as she pet her mouse's head with a single finger, the rodent's long whiskers peering out of her sleeve.

Lauren took Bethany's hand and walked her towards the large Mother oak. August's throat tugged at the memory of Margaret cowering in pain, protected by this very tree after the fire. Tonight the oak sparkled, its roots ran glittering with glowing fungi. "Bethany Young, tonight we bring you into our circle of sisters," said Lauren, sweeping her arm around the women.

The duck quacked, the squirrel chirped, the crow flapped its wings, the mouse squeaked, and the badger grunted solemnly. "Bethany, we welcome you into your ancestral chain. We bring you in as a sister, one who nurtures and supports our community and our Mother," said Lauren, helping Bethany lie down among the oak's roots.

Bethany lay on her back and looked up at the ancient branches protecting her from above, her black dress clinging to her body. *What the actual fuck?* August marvelled as tiny butter fungi rapidly sprouted. Each mushroom steadily rose from the bark surrounding Bethany's head. A living headpiece of sparkling fungi twisted through her hair, dusted her ears, and circled her forehead. The girl was now linked to the soil, to her sisters, and to her new Mother.

Hazel rose and slowly walked across the circle to sit at Bethany's bare feet. She gave a small chirp and the women in circle bowed their heads.

Suddenly, August noticed each Carer wore their own headpiece of fungi. The mistaken strands of silver embroidery were mycelium. These fungal threads stretched across dark chests, crawled up necks, and wove through hair, each Carer gifted with their own unique headpiece.

Lauren, her headpiece filled with sparkling gall fungi continued. "Bethany, being in ceremony with your sisters, you recognize that the threads connect us to our past, our present, and our future. As a Carer, you will continue to learn the ways of the Mother. You will promise to care, protect, and support the Mother Network."

Each Carer raised her arms to the canopy. Bethany, her eyes softened with tears, lifted her arms to the Mother oak.

They all spoke out in unison. "We promise to care, protect, and support the Mother Network."

As the rallying cry faded, Bethany rose and the women crowded her with hugs, welcoming her into their sisterhood. August held a deep warmth and love for everything around her. She smiled. *It's like Margaret's here with us.*

THIRTY-EIGHT
AUGUST

Bethany raised her hand, blocking out the late evening sun pouring over the cottage. "I'll see you for swimming in a bit," she said, picking yarrow from the medicinal garden.

The afternoon light was warm, the air calm, the rocks cool under August's feet, the wicker basket solid in her hand.

The granite stone beside the swimming hole was firm beneath her feet. She undid the knots at each shoulder of her summer dress and let it fall to her feet. A light breeze blew over her stomach and down her thighs.

August raised her arms over her head, her body stretching towards the treetops, and took a deep breath. "I am here. I am alive. I am enough," she declared, then stepped out of her dress and dropped into the pool.

August floated. Her buoyant body lay on the water and relaxed. Inhaling a deep breath into her lungs, she sensed her body rise to meet the sky and, with an outward breath, let her body sink back into the watery softness. She played with her breath and her body, the water lapping in gentle, cooling waves.

Stroking across the surface of the pool, August felt the liquid glide against her body. She stopped and submerged her head, listening to the bubbles deep beneath. When she broke the surface she yelled, "OOOOOOOO!" emptying her lungs and laughing. August recognised connection to this world, a tethering to this place. *I am here*, she whispered to herself. *I am me and all those lists can fuck off*.

Climbing out of the pool, August sat beside her basket. She rang the water from her long raven hair flecked with lengthening silver threads, beads of water trickled down her back. There was a rhythm to the water, a peace and lightness that welled in her body after a swim. The water let August ground herself in the present.

She used this gift every day. When an item screamed at her, demanded to be added to her list she'd scan her surroundings for something to grip: *Well, hello, beautiful buttercup. Louisa-Ray's smile. Grace's gurgle. Worn grey paint on a wooden cup. Warm dirt under my feet. The clean, crisp water from the stream. Margaret's smile.* She'd pull herself back to the now, full of gratitude.

After wiping her wet hands, she grabbed the Family Hive, pushing the cork stopper with her thumb. She raised the cool stone bottle to her mouth and took a sip, her moist palm pressing against the pottery. The sadly familiar ache of loss and love welled up in her heart. *That's just how I feel here: all mixed up, but also at peace.* August took another sip and placed the bottle back into the basket.

A shock ran through her feet and tingled each hair on her body. A rush of air filled August's ears. She balanced herself with one hand against the rock beneath her body. Her breath raced, the clinging water drops on her bare toes almost sizzled. A soft, rhythmic voice came to her mind: *You are here. You are there. You are everywhere.*

With a rush of adrenaline, August shook. She recognized that voice. That beautiful, soft cadence could only be Margaret.

"Margaret?"

August waited for a reply.

"Margaret, are you there?"

I am, August. I am now one with the Mother. I have always been with you. Only now can I be heard. August stood up frantically, knocking over the basket, beer pooling onto the granite, weaving its way down to the water's edge. "What? You've always been with me? What does that even mean?"

Her words echoed across the swimming hole; the burst of air in her ears subsided. She squeezed her lips, listening intently. She picked up the odd flutter of bat wings, the gentle whoosh of the afternoon breeze caressing the oak leaves. Then everything faded into white.

THIRTY-NINE
AUGUST

August was nauseous as the whiteout dissolved from her eyes. She sensed her feet on the ground, her arms resting on a table, and listened to a loud hum she'd not heard for years.

And there, in front of her face, was Andrew. She froze. *Is this my dream life? Am I dreaming right now?* She took a deep breath to control her shaking.

She touched the tough denim on the thighs of her vintage jeans. Her Doc Marten boots felt light on her feet. Great wafts of strong florals and industrial cleaner flooded her nose.

"August, are you okay?" asked Andrew, looking up from his phone, watching her with a quizzical face. "You look... odd."

August looked at the pint of beer in her hand, her wet palm touching the cool glass. *I fucking knew it!* thought August. Then said out loud, "I FUCKING KNEW IT!" and slammed the table with her hand.

Everyone in the pub stopped talking. August grimaced

in the silence and said, "Apologies," in a light voice, raising her glass to the room. *Here's hoping they think I've over celebrated.* A few of her tour mates raised their pints in a toast, and the chatter started again.

August put the pint glass back down on the table. "What is wrong with you?" asked Andrew anxiously.

"Oh," she looked up, "I'm sorry," she whispered. *What am I supposed to do? I'm back home? My other home? Will I be staying here?* And then Ripley's smile, her wavy blonde hair flowing over her shoulders, her stuffed panda flooded back. "Ripley," she said out loud. A surge of electrical love overloaded her system. Her hands shook against the table, tiny taps sent out an SOS as she realized, *I haven't abandoned her!*

"Are you *sure* you're okay?" asked Andrew. He leant towards August across the table, his pine-scented bodywash filled her nose. August was unsure what to say as the humming in her body subsided. Andrew sighed and took off his black-framed glasses, two red divots appearing along his nose bridge. August watched Andrew try to pull the stress and strain of their lives from his face, push it away with his fingertips, massage it out his pores. "I know this is hard. This is really hard. Our everyday lives are hard," he said, rubbing his nose, his eyes closed.

Anxiety surged through August as Andrew said the words, "everyday lives." The schedules, the doctors' appointments, the cat food orders, the grocery planning. The list roared with a second life, jamming her brain. *Stop, you can stop this.* She searched for her tethers: the electric hum of the overhead lights, her feet in her soft socks, the stubble on Andrew's chin.

The pulsing in her body stopped. And right then, August recognised Andrew would never help her with her lists. This wasn't right. This world wasn't in balance and wouldn't be until she made some changes. August quickly reached out for Andrew's hand, which held his phone. "What is it?" he asked as she placed her hand on his. Everything flooded back: the company, the problems, their marriage, their fights, the pointlessness of it all. She gently took the phone from his fingers and placed it on the table. "Andrew, we both know this isn't working, right?"

Andrew looked around awkwardly. August counted in her head: *one Mississippi, two Mississippi, three Mississippi. Give him the space he needs to answer.* Eventually he said softly, "I know."

They both looked at their beers as August sensed a craving to run, to escape. *I want to go back to Louisa-Ray's hugs, and the cottage, and Bethany,* but then it hit her. She was back here. Right here in a world with Ripley. *Oh, Ripley...*

"We're going to have to tell Ripley," August said quietly and waited again.

She turned the cool glass of beer in her hand, her fingertips moving beads of condensation around the surface. *How are these worlds connected? Will I jump again? And does –*

Andrew cut off her off with a soft, "Yeah, we will tell Ripley." A pause and then, "But maybe we should wait until after the holiday? Give her one last family vacation?"

August's body softened. *He loves her so much.* "Andrew, I get that you want to protect Ripley and her last holiday, but I think we should just rip off the Band-Aid. At least here we have more time to talk and answer her questions. What do you think?"

"Yeah, I suppose that's true. We'll have more time here. There's six days left."

"Take the Long Way Home" by Supertramp played on the pub's speakers. *Pretty fucking fitting. Thank you, Mother.*

"Now," she said gently to Andrew, "let's go get our darling Ripley and plan how to share our changing family news."

FORTY
AUGUST

August couldn't stop smiling at Ripley. For the first three days of her return, August would randomly grab her little girl with a kissy-monster attack. Those physical impulses had softened, but she couldn't stop gazing, hoarding the oxytocin bursts she'd missed.

Ripley sat in the coffee shop next to Andrew. Her legs dangled, her bright blue rain boots banging against the bench seat.

"Do you have any questions?" asked Andrew, palming his greying chin stubble, brushing it over and over, his calming meditation.

Ripley's two front teeth hung over her bottom lip, resting across the indent they'd created. *Don't tell her to put her lips together.*

"Not really," said Ripley casually and then with more energy, "Can I have my brownie now?"

August smiled with relief. The divorce conversation hadn't been terrible, awkward but not terrible. Ripley appeared fine; the most important thing to her was still dessert.

"Sure, Ripley, I'll grab it," said Andrew, rapidly standing, clutching his phone.

August watched Ripley gaze around the small coffee shop, scanning the vibrantly coloured prints hung in white frames, banging her boots rhythmically. August reached for Ripley's hand over the round table, the little fingers sticky and heavy in August's. "Poppet, I just want you to understand that your dad and I will never stop loving you. And we'll never stop being your parents."

Ripley looked at August, titled her head, her blonde bangs grazing her blue eyes. "Okay, Mum."

"Are you actually okay?"

"I'm okay… I don't feel sick, but I am tired."

"Yeah, big feelings use a lot of energy and can leave us really tired."

"Yeah, big feelings."

A café chair scraped the floor, causing Ripley and August to turn. A sixtyish woman with a shining yellow mackintosh pushed her chair back under the table with a second tooth clenching squeal. "Squeeeeeeeeeeeee," said Ripley, imitating the noise.

August laughed, then softly reminded Ripley that not everyone in the busy café would appreciate the joke. Ripley drummed her fingers on the table, then suddenly stopped banging her legs, her fingers settled. August waited.

"Mum?"

"Yes, sweetheart."

"What happened to… you?"

"That's a hard question to answer. Things happen all

the time to families. We all change and grow, and sometimes that's means growing apart."

"That's not what I mean." Ripley unclamped her front teeth from her lip. "You're different. What did you do?" August's body vibrated with panic. "You're... happy," Ripley finished.

Ease overtook August's limbs. "You know what, Ripley? You're right. I am happy." She leant over and whispered, "You're the only one who's noticed." August squeezed her hand. "I love you."

Ripley squealed, "Oh, look, Dad's got lots of brownies!"

Ripley pulled her tacky fingers from August's palm and reached out to Andrew, who was returning with three dark brownies on a plate. "I figured we each needed a brownie," he said, putting the plate down, narrowly avoiding Ripley's speedy grab for the closest bar. "And I ordered us each another flat white," he added, smiling softly at August.

August sat back in her chair as Ripley caked her lips and fingernails with dark sugar and chocolate. Andrew took a large bite of his brownie, small crumbles catching in his short beard. *You're okay. Ripley is okay. Andrew is okay. We're okay.* August knew a mountain of questions, uncertainty, and adjustments would show in their future, but for now everyone was alright.

As Ripley took the last bite of her brownie, sighing in delight, August wondered what Ripley saw in her, that nobody else had noticed.

On the flight home to Victoria, Ripley slept, her pyjama legs curled in her seat. August stroked Ripley's blonde hair, cradling the little crown on her lap. *My sweet girl. I made it home to you.*

"Okay," said Andrew, sipping red wine from a tiny plastic cup as he looked at his laptop. "I think we've covered the major things. Custody and parenting arrangements. Financial support and expenses. Living arrangements and property. We haven't finished the section on communications and boundaries, but I'm beat."

"Yeah. Let's finish that off when we get home. And speaking of communications and boundaries, we didn't fight once doing our divorce list," added August.

"Yeah," said Andrew quietly.

August placed her hand around Andrew's arm, his fingers on his keyboard, the Google document glowing in the dim cabin. "We had to do this. You know that, right?"

"Yeah," said Andrew. "But I can't help feeling like we failed, that I failed at marriage."

"We both failed," August admitted. "But I think that's okay. We're learning. One thing we both want is the best for Ripley."

"You're right. We do want the best for Ripley." A pause, then, "August?"

"Yeah?"

"You're a great mom, just in case I haven't said it recently."

"Well, Andrew, you're also a great dad. In case I haven't said it recently," said August with a smile.

Andrew took a last gulp of his wine and shut the laptop. "Okay, good enough for now. I'm gonna watch some crappy action movie."

"Okay. I'm gonna try and sleep a bit."

As Andrew scrolled the in-flight movie list, August bent down and breathed in Ripley's unique smell, the scent her daughter arrived with into the birthing room. Just then, the never-ending list tried to make itself understood with a barrage of thoughts about divorce planning. August spoke sternly to herself: *We're done with fucking lists! We're focusing on now.* The hum of the airplane. Ripley's soft skin beneath my fingers. Joy tingling my body… *We're okay*.

FORTY-ONE
AUGUST

August sat on the front porch of her duplex, the cedar planks already warm under her feet, and tenderly admired the three-hundred-year-old Gary oak in her new neighbour's yard.

Their family dynamic was building a different rhythm. Ripley spent one week at Andrew's, one week with her. Rocking between parents, Ripley was riding this wave with grace and sometimes tears. But mostly they managed.

August stretched her arms to the sky, blinking into the morning sunshine. *It's a perfect swimming day.* Then looked down at her list. The realities of divorce, the new routines and decisions, meant lists were unavoidable.

August stepped from the deck through her sliding door into the kitchen, her piece of paper in hand. The new-to-me fridge hummed as she slapped the list to the fridge. Held it there with a ladybug magnet Ripley made in kindergarten. "And that's where you'll stay!" said August confidently, arms on her hips, almost daring the list to migrate back to her mind.

Ripley hummed softly to herself as she read her graphic novel. The rock of the Gorge waterway was warm under August's legs and bare feet.

The local rocky hangout quieted as caregivers packed up half-eaten sandwiches and convinced toddlers to put on shoes so they could go home for dinner. Tabatha texted to say she was on her way to meet them. She'd just "suited up!"

The air was warm, and the moment calm. A heron stood on one leg in the bay, watching the kayakers and canoes overloaded with sunscreened faces and life jackets. The company sale was still under an NDA and, yes, the lawyers were still arguing over minutiae items, but that didn't matter anymore. *Margaret, you'd love it here*, thought August.

August's second life had reshaped her first. Her time with Margaret, Louisa-Ray, Hugh, Angus, Grace, and Bethany had snipped away the tangled threads and interwoven lists that strangled her life with Ripley. The strong remaining threads revealed a beautiful and extraordinary life: one that had always been there.

August closed her eyes, took a deep breath, and sighed. When she opened her lids, Ripley stood right in front of her, summer freckles splattered across her nose. "Mum, guess what just happened in the book?"

"What happened? Was it exciting?" She stood up and took Ripley's hand in hers. "Tell me about it while we have a swim."

AUGUST

They scrambled down the rocks and, with squeals, plunged into the cold water. Their bodies settled as the shock of the coolness dissolved. Floating on their backs, they watched the soft clouds rush past on coastal air. "We're like otters," said Ripley, grabbing August's hand. *My heart is full*, thought August, Ripley's fingers meshed with hers.

After their dip, they sat on the rock, knees bent, eating handfuls of salt and pepper chips. "Mum?" asked Ripley.

"Yes."

"It's really beautiful here, isn't it?"

"You're not wrong poppet. It really is. We're so lucky to live here," said August, reaching for Ripley's hand.

They sat there, connected in deep contentment as a tiny boat passed their outcropping, a single woman with a blue hat rowed in strong, smooth sculls.

August detected a warming in her toes, then a tremendous flash of adrenaline shot through her body. Nausea rose in her throat, her eyesight blurred, the world morphed into a tie-dye T-shirt. *Oh fuck, here we go again... and I think this time Ripley's coming with me.*

Book Two of the Thread Traveller series coming October 2026!

Ripley and August travel to a third parallel dimension, where August discovers her birth family and learns why she jumps realities.

THE NEVER-ENDING TO-DO LIST

Hi, reader, I bet you feel the heavy load of invisible labour, or as I call it, the never-ending to-do list. You are not alone!

The Never-Ending To-Do List:

- Must order new refill bottle of hand sanitizer from Nezza Naturals.
- Book couples counselling session.
- Order a new straw for Ripley's water bottle.
- Book a pedicure so my feet don't look so gross.
- Put more simple syrup in the feeder, so the hummingbirds don't die while we're on holiday.
- Order more detangler.
- Double-check what's covered by our travel insurance.
- Make doctor's appointment and get a full physical.

- Book the arborist to assess the sickly cedar.
- Listen to *The Body Is Not an Apology* on Audible
- Must do more pigeon pose; these hips are tight!
- Order more Joni pads for perimenopause emergencies.
- Replace the full caffeine coffee with half caf.
- Do more thoracic yoga.
- Create New To-Do List: Get Home.

Get Home Never-Ending To-Do List:

- See what I can find at the great house.
- See if these boots might help me get home.
- Try other foods, like turnip to see if they send me home.
- Will gall fungi take me home?
- Is perimenopause causing my travel?
- Is the gold cap blue mushroom my way home?
- Make beer and get home!
- Figure out how to talk to the Mother.
- Write out the changed process for Hugh.
- Scrap the list — and live right now!

BURN THE LIST!

ALL THE THANK YOU'S

Dear reader,

Hello to the lovely eyes reading this right now! **Thank you** for spending time with me and supporting this happy / terrified / exhausted author nervously publishing her debut novel.

The moment I shared August, Margaret and the Thread Carers with you, the story became yours as well. In fact, I think it's even better now that you're here with me.

Your Review Makes A Difference!

Starting my publishing house, Salt Line Press, means reviews and recommendations are the mycelium that helps others discover this novel.

Please leave a review to help someone else travel with August to meet Margaret:

Leave a review - thank you!

If you *really loved* the book, please consider buying a copy and gifting it to a friend, or dropping it into a little free library.

Leave A Review and Win A Prize Pack

I want to *thank you* for taking the time to read my book and then write a review. Visit my page below and upload your review screenshot. Every reviewer is entered to win a seasonal prize pack from wonderful creatives: illustrators, potters, jewellers and more.

Win a prize pack of creative goodies

Want a sneak peek of where August and Ripley end up in book two? I send out a monthly newsletter that promises ridiculous book TikTok's, threaded with longer articles on midlife and insights into my writing or not-writing (which is really watching bad tv and eating chocolate in bed).

Sign up for my monthly newsletter

So Many Thanks

There have been *many* people over my 49 years who've supported, loved and challenged me to write. Deep breath...

Firstly, I have to thank my writing buddy, Alyssa. She and I wrote our debut novels together. Alyssa gifted me the motivation to keep going with my first and second drafts. Thank you Alyssa!

To all my beta readers—Jeff, Michelle, Dwight, Mij, and Matt—thank you for being so thoughtful with your feedback to this shaky first time writer. xo

Michelle, my wonderful book editor. Thank you for helping with my pacing, uncovering the true themes, and giving me the confidence to keep going. I cannot wait to work with you on the second book.

My copy editor Jenny. You made this book more consistent, smooth, and lighter. Thank you for your red pen :)

To my board game group: thank you for listening to me bang on about my book, for understanding when I canceled because I was on deadline, and keeping my brain young with **very** complicated board games.

To my female writer's group - I can't wait to read your future books. I believe in you. xo

Mark, you demanded that I get off my ass and "finally write the book you've always talked about." Thanks for that.

I have to thank my aunt for hot Ubering me around Kent and providing me with a space to write and rest in Faversham. Much of the inspiration for this book came from my time with you. I love you.

Thank you to my friend Ann, who gave me the idea of "what if perimenopause was actually the thing that caused the traveling?" Genius idea! I love you and June.

Hannah, I knew you were the perfect person to bring my cover to life. I was not wrong! Thank you for all your care, attention and creativity.

Michelle, I couldn't do any of this without you. Thank you for our drives and for listening to me rant about character holes, plus giving me confidence and support when I felt myself failing. You're my best bud.

My daughter Ada, thank you for inspiring me and reminding me that creativity doesn't disappear with age — we just have to let it out. I love you, poppet.

Mij, you're it! I can't wait to read your debut. Thank you for all the encouragement. I love you!

Anna N., what would I do without all our laughs. Thank you for all for making me pee myself with laughter!

To Aimee, Reid, Chris, David, Geri, Lissy, Steve and all the Mitchells for coming into my life. I'm so happy to be a part of your family.

Thank you to my mom for teaching me that being different is totally okay. I carry that torch proudly, along with our Monk and Lavelle family stories. I love you. Kirk, I'm ready to celebrate with a mojito!

Thank you to my dad for instilling a love of books; *Swallows and Amazons* and *Hitchhiker's Guide to the Galaxy* will always remind me of you. Thanks for your support of my *many* endeavours. I love you.

A special thank you to my brother for always letting me *be myself*. He's always accepted me for who I am, with all my flaws, and been okay with them — in fact, even celebrated my differences, to the annoyance of others. Thank you, Matt. You're the best brother ever. I love you.

And to my co-founder, co-parent and co-partner, Jeff. I could not have written this book without you. Not only have you given me the space and time to write, market, build my publishing house, and record my audiobook, you've gently pressured me with loving kindness to keep going when I wanted to stop. You always believed, from when we met in 2001, that I would write a book. This is for you.

To every person in my life—whether family, friend, Goodreads buddy, Kiwi family, colleague, neighbour, or team member—who asked how my book was going, thank you! You don't know how much it kept me on track. This ADHD brain needed all the encouragement.

To every female founder out there: I see how hard you work, how you're doing it all and often feel you're getting it wrong. That's okay. I believe in you.

Thank you to my University of Victoria Writing Professors Lorna Crozier, Jack Hodgins, Stephen Osborne and Patrick Lane; here I am, twenty-five years later, still hearing their voices guide me through my prose. Thank you.

I want to thank the authors who inspired me to be a writer: Margaret Atwood, Michael Ondaatje, Douglas Adams, John Wyndham, P.D. James, Terry Pratchett and Anne McCaffrey. And thank you to every librarian who gave me a book that sucked me into another world.

Thank you Mrs. McGee, Mrs. McCoy and Miss Morin. These wonderful English teachers gave me confidence in my voice and love of stories. And to all my other junior high and high-school teachers thank you for giving me a safe and warm place to "grow up": Mr. Bernard, Mr. Portrais, Mr. Hughes, Mr. Forrester, Mrs. Bedard, Mr. Parnell, and Madame Senkow.

Key places inspired me to write this novel: The town of Faversham and the surrounding Kentish hop fields, the Maison Dieu, the Franciscan Gardens of Canterbury, and Shepeard Neame opened up the world of ale wives and kicked off this entire book.

Thank you to the independent bookshops in Victoria: Munro's Books, Russell Books, Ivy's Book Shop, Tanner's Books and Bolen Books.

Thank you to beautiful Vancouver Island, this magical Turtle Island, which inspires me every time I take a step or swim in the Salish Sea.

I always wanted to be a writer. And now, 49 years later, **I AM**.

With gratitude and excitement for what's to come,

Annabel, xoxo

Ps. To all my ladies tired of all the societal expectations, it's your turn to shine. Go out there, do it, and then come back to tell me *all* about it.

Let's collaborate!

One of my book goals is to inspire creativity in others. We all need to resist or rally in our own unique and creative ways. If you want to collaborate or see what collaborations are in the works, get in touch.

Come and creatively collaborate with me

ABOUT ANNABEL

Annabel originally studied creative writing at the University of Victoria in her 20s, when she fell into her own alternate dimension, the world of tech. After being hired as employee number 11 at Abebooks.com, an online marketplace for rare, used and out-of-print books, Annabel witnessed how the internet could connect people and help independent, used bookstores thrive.

Annabel followed her desire to build community and collaboration with her husband. They founded two global technology startups and after living in New Zealand and

L.A. they settled back on Vancouver Island to be close to their families.

In early 2022, at age 46, Annabel realised the speculative fiction novel she kept putting off needed a chance to grow. She resigned her Chief Marketing Officer position and began her journey as an authorpreneur, bringing her tech, marketing and community skills to forming Salt Line Press - a new independent publishing house focused on stories of transformation, particularly for women in midlife.

Annabel's debut novel, Thread Traveller, was inspired by the idea that perimenopause should be seen as a positive powerful stage, even reality busting.

Annabel lives in Victoria, B.C. with her husband, daughter and cat, Hubble. When she's not typing, or reading, she's sewing her own garments and swimming every chance she can in the Salish Sea.

www.ingramcontent.com/pod-product-compliance
Ingram Content Group UK Ltd.
Pitfield, Milton Keynes, MK11 3LW, UK
UKHW040904011025
463460UK00002B/29